4-EVER MINE

4-EVER, BOOK 2

JAYNE RYLON

HAPPY ENDINGS PUBLISHING

ABOUT THE BOOK

A year after Andi claimed her three smoking hot roommates for her own, she's finally emerging from a blissful haze of lust long enough to look around and realize things aren't quite as amazing as they could be.

While she and her boyfriends have an incredible sex life, they haven't fully embraced their relationship in public. When someone puts one and three together—outing them from the polyamorous closet—they have to decide where to go next.

Will they be able to stay together or will reality tear them apart?

ADDITIONAL INFORMATION

Sign up for the Naughty News for contests, release updates, news, appearance information, sneak peek excerpts, reading-themed apparel deals, and more. www.jaynerylon.com/newsletter

Shop for autographed books, reading-themed apparel, goodies, and more www.jaynerylon.com/shop

A complete list of Jayne's books can be found at www.jaynerylon.com/books

1

———

Andi roused from a very pleasant, very naughty dream to an even more mind-blowing reality. A warm hand brushed her hair aside and someone placed a kiss on her bare shoulder before crawling into bed with her. The instant the man wrapped himself around her, she knew which of her three boyfriends it was—Reed.

"Mmm." She cuddled against him. If her ass brushed his groin long enough to make his cock harden, she couldn't be sad about that. "Gooooooood morning."

"It's about to be." He ran his hand from her hip up her side until he could cup her breast in his palm. He had a thing for her chest that she didn't mind indulging. In fact, Andi intentionally squirmed in his hold, angling her torso so he had better access to her skin, which was warm and supple from being nestled under the duvet of the bed she often shared with her roommates-turned-lovers.

She blinked, waking up more by the second. Reed's bold caresses were better than her precious Columbian coffee at drawing her into the land of the living. "Is it just you?"

"Yeah. Simon had an early practice with the team and Cooper is observing his boss try a case before his classes today. Disappointed?"

"Never." She reached up and drew his face to hers so she could prove it with a scorching kiss. Reed tried to be gentle and playful, but he wasn't Simon. He could only go a few seconds before his dominant instincts kicked in and he wrested control from her.

She didn't mind in the least.

Reed showed her what she'd been missing while he'd been out of town negotiating with suppliers for his fledgling medical supply business. She was glad to have him here with her again. While neither Cooper nor Simon had let her get too lonely, Reed brought his own special flavor to their mix. Without it, she didn't feel complete.

Same went when either of the other two were gone.

Did that make her selfish? Probably, but she was learning to embrace her desires instead of apologizing for them.

"Damn, Andi. I'm so glad to be home." Reed rolled on top of her, bracing himself on his forearms so he wouldn't squish her with his much larger body. The gesture only highlighted his muscular arms and the bulk of his quads, which knotted against her thighs.

She ran her hands up and down his biceps, reassuring herself—and him—that they were together again.

"You know, if the other two guys weren't here with you, I'd never be able to do my job," he whispered in between attacking her neck with feverish kisses. "I love knowing they're taking care of you. That you're safe and happy while I'm handling business."

"But it's never the same without you. Or any of them." She hugged Reed, confident he wouldn't be jealous that she'd admitted it. "Welcome home."

He grinned. "I'm not quite there yet, but I will be soon."

Reed took a moment to get rid of his pants, then assumed his original position. This time, his cock sat on her belly while he made out with her some more. Her hands wandered down his powerful back to his ass, then squeezed, trying to direct him.

Which she should have guessed would backfire.

"Don't make me tie you up." He growled against her chest, above her breast, as he nipped the flesh there. "We're going to do this my way. On my schedule. That seems only fair since you've been getting some, but I haven't."

"What if I like it when you tie me up?" She wasn't teasing. Or maybe she was intentionally prodding him in the hopes he'd follow through on his threats. Andi had come to adore being at his mercy. It was one of the things they had in common that the other two of her lovers didn't necessarily share.

Something that was their own.

She loved fulfilling each of their particular needs, as they did for her—without judgment, fear, or hesitation.

"Well, then that's entirely different." Reed flashed a brilliant smile in her direction. He reached down to pluck his recently discarded shirt from the floor without getting off of her for even an instant. In fact, he seemed to let himself settle onto her more fully, impressing his entire body into hers.

"Mmm," she purred as she rubbed upward against him, fusing their torsos as completely as possible. It hadn't been so long ago that this was new and forbidden territory for them. After a year, she felt as comfortable fucking him as she did hanging out on the couch, or studying for difficult exams when they'd been college roommates.

Still, the thrill lingered. Especially when he got in a mood like this.

Reed rolled his T-shirt until it looked more like a short length of rope than something capable of covering his broad shoulders and sculpted back. He held the length in his fists and gave her that look. The one that melted her panties, when she was wearing any.

"Put your hands over your head. Now."

She complied instantly.

He took his time winding the soft material, which smelled of him, around her wrists, knowing she loved the anticipation of the binding nearly as much as the act itself. And when he finally drew his simple knot tight, trapping her arms together, she shivered.

"You really do love that, don't you?" He kissed the tip of her nose before trailing his hand down the center of her body, directly to her pussy. His message was clear. Her entire body was on display, his to do with whatever he pleased.

Andi nodded, biting her lower lip to keep from screaming when his palm cupped her mound and his middle finger traced her slit.

"Damn straight you do. You're soaked already." He bent then, filling his mouth with her nipple, using his tongue to toy with it until it was rock-hard and aching. As he did, he inserted his finger into her, slowly boring deeper as he coated himself with her arousal.

After being completely spoiled by three men and their impressive cocks, a finger wasn't going to hold her over for long. Andi whimpered and tried to raise her pelvis in an attempt to force Reed deeper.

"You need more?" he asked, knowing full well she did. They both did.

"Please, Reed."

"That's better." He grinned before nipping the pebbled tip of her breast and sliding over to give her other one the same treatment. "Now I'm starting to think you really did miss me."

"Fuck me and I'll show you just how much I love your cock, Reed." Andi wasn't sure when she'd grown bold enough to talk to him like that. It had happened slowly, over the course of the past twelve months.

He grinned. While he clearly enjoyed knowing she could take what he was dishing out plus give as good as she got, when she displayed that same sexual directness with the other guys, it blew them away. Simon especially seemed to like it when she got aggressive, demanded satisfaction, and wrested power from him.

Being with Reed made her a better lover for her other lovers.

Although the times the four of them had sex together were some of her favorite escapades, she adored their individual relationships as well. Their unique dynamic worked for them. More than worked.

Andi was thriving.

She spread her legs in invitation.

"Is this what you want?" Reed knelt between her thighs, raising his torso far enough that she could see him fisting his cock, pumping the last bit of stiffness into it that he'd need to penetrate the rings of muscle at her entrance, which were tense with expectation.

She nodded.

"Say it. Ask for it," he directed.

"Please give me your cock. I want to feel it deep inside me. Spreading me open and making me come so hard that you can't help but join me," she murmured.

"Damn, Andi. You're getting awfully good at that."

She winked.

He responded by feeding his cock into her pussy, inch by inch.

There. Now he was truly home.

"Shit. Yes. I missed you so much." He grunted as he seated himself fully within her. Only when he'd locked them together did he pause to make love to her mouth with his own. Then it seemed like he couldn't get enough.

Reed deepened the contact of their lips and ransacked her mouth with his tongue.

All she could do was accept the onslaught of pleasure. As if to remind her, he leaned on her bound hands, which raised her chest, grinding it against his. The pounding of his heart on her breast startled her.

She opened her eyes and stared into his as he showed her just how much she could impact him. His cock jerked within her, despite the fact that he hadn't started moving and simply held her impaled on his thick shaft.

Andi clenched around him, massaging him with her pussy. When he groaned, she smirked.

"Oh, you think that's funny?" he growled.

She nodded and did it again.

His eyes were in danger of rolling back in his head, or at least she thought they were. But she didn't get the best view because just then he pulled out of her, making her gasp at the sudden emptiness. "No, come back. I'll be good, I promise."

Reed chuckled. "Don't worry. I'm not going far."

He wrapped his arm around her waist and rotated her so that her face was buried in her pillow. She knew better than to move her arms from over her head. That might have been the only thing that kept her on his good side.

Whatever tricks she tried to play on Reed, he'd always one-up her. She loved that she could do anything she liked, and he'd always conquer her again. He could handle all of her. She braced herself, prepared for a spank or two dozen, but when his hand landed on her ass it wasn't to slap it. She tried not to be disappointed.

No, he killed her with sweet caresses she would have expected from Cooper, not Reed.

Who was this man?

When she peeked over his shoulder, she found Reed after all. This time he did send sparks of delicious heat through her ass with his hand. "Did I tell you to turn around?"

"No, sir." She whipped her head forward again.

"You tease me, I tease you." He trailed a single finger down her crack, then flicked it over her clit.

Andi moaned and spread her knees wider.

He laughed. "We'll see how long you want more for."

When she would have asked what he meant, he answered by showing her. Reed rolled to his back on the bed, between her legs, and drew her down so he could bury his face in her pussy. He wasn't messing around.

Instead, he went straight to suckling her clit with the exact amount of pressure she preferred. He wasn't trying to draw things out. He was trying to make her come. At least that's what she thought until her thighs trembled on either side of his neck and her channel began to clench around the fingers he'd worked back inside her.

At the exact moment she screamed his name, he stopped.

"No!" she shouted, and kicked her feet.

Reed's big palm came down on her ass then. He mumbled against her soaked flesh, "Not so fast."

"Please," Andi begged. She wasn't sure exactly what words came out of her then. Whatever they were, they must have been effective. Reed took up where he'd left off, bringing her to the very edge again before raking his teeth over her clit and stealing the urgency from her gathering muscles.

He hummed against her pussy, then started again.

Andi lost track of how many times he brought her to the brink of orgasm. All she knew was that if she didn't have him soon, she would die. Or beg him to call one of the other guys home to do the job for him.

She sagged against the bed, unable to hold herself up when every molecule of her being was focused on the pulsing between her legs. Only then did she realize Reed had moved. Where was he? She didn't dare peek.

Couldn't stand it if he delayed her release any longer.

"That's better," he crooned from behind her as he aligned their bodies, her ass to his pelvis. "This time, we'll come together. Deal?"

Andi could only nod, unable to speak if it wasn't to scream his name.

Reed bent over her, his strong chest blanketing her back. The fingers of one of his hands wrapped carefully around her throat while the other aimed his cock at her core. He rubbed the blunt tip up and down her slit, gliding against her clit several times before notching it at her entrance.

It took every shred of willpower she possessed not to rock back and force him inside. It was worth it when he plunged into her, claiming her with a single fluid stroke that would have been impossible until he'd nearly drowned himself to ensure she was wild with ecstasy.

"Yes!" he shouted. "Fuck, yes. You're so tight and hot on my cock."

Andi shuddered, already on the verge of exploding.

"I knew I'd never last long. Even after a few days, I forget how incredible it is to be with you like this. And when my dick is back in this pretty pussy, all I want to do is flood it with my come so you know who you belong to." Reed grunted as he fucked her. Hard. "Us. You belong to *us*."

She did.

And her body prepared to admit it.

Andi's toes curled and she bit the T-shirt binding her hands to keep herself grounded.

"You're ready to come? With me?" Reed rasped against her neck—grazing it with his teeth—ensuring that even if she hadn't been before, she would be then.

She nodded and whimpered under the pressure of holding back her orgasm. Until he freed her from the burden.

"Do it. Now." He reached one hand beneath her and rubbed her clit as he pounded into her, slapping her ass with his abs on every lunge. The instant she shattered, she heard him curse and groan. He locked deep within her, then jerked as his hips twitched, pumping every bit of his come into her.

Andi smiled around his shirt, satisfied to the marrow

of her bones. Her body kept spasming, drawing out Reed's own bliss, but nothing could compare to the joy in her heart, knowing how well she'd pleased him.

How completely she could take care of all three of her men.

She sighed as she indulged in the aftershocks of her climax while Reed smooshed her into the mattress. He shifted only slightly once his cock softened enough to slip from her body, then held her close as he started to snore.

Good thing her alarm was still set or she'd be late to work for sure.

2

—————

"Can you believe it's been a year since we started living together?" Andi asked Simon, Reed, and Cooper as they sat around their dining room table eating brunch together the next morning. It was rare—even on a Saturday—that they were all home and available at the same time given their dedication to their budding careers, continuing education, and trying to align four busy schedules.

"Andi, you're way better at math than me," Simon teased, making his other roommates snort at that gross understatement. Andi might have been his super-cute girlfriend, but she was also a brilliant chemist. "So you should know we moved in together *five* years ago."

She laughed, then flung a chunk of waffle at him. He leaned in and snapped it out of midair, making her crack up even more. Sure, he was the most playful of her roommates-turned-lovers, but he knew she took him seriously when it counted.

Andi continued her train of thought aloud. "Yeah, but

that was before we used to sleep together. It hardly counts."

"True. You've never really *lived* until you've had a ménage." Of course Cooper had caught her meaning right away. They had some special psychic mind-meld that Simon was sometimes jealous of. For like a split second, before he got over it. He and Andi had an emotional bond. She and Cooper had a mental one. Her and Reed...well, that was over-the-top physical.

Simon should know. As a sports medicine professional, he'd given her plenty of massages, helping to loosen her lean muscles after Reed had worn her out.

Andi beamed. She came alive when all of them were together.

Her mood and their attention guaranteed they were about to have an insanely good weekend. That is, if Reed and his big ideas didn't fuck things up.

Simon wasn't sure their plan would work. At all. But he trusted Reed and Cooper's judgment when it came to important matters. They both had voted that Andi would love their surprise. He prayed they were right. It had been a while since she'd had one of her nightmares, though she still got spooked sometimes if he came up behind her without making a racket and she would always turn her cell phone flashlight on if she had to get up during the night.

It hurt him to see even those minor changes in her. She'd never been afraid before the disaster last year. Which was why revisiting that turbulent time in their past seemed dangerous to him. Maybe he just hated to think about it himself. They had almost ended up torn apart.

What would his life be like without Andi? Or his other roommates?

Incomplete. That's what it would be. Their arrangement might not be conventional, but it suited them—each of them individually, and all of them as a whole—perfectly.

Hopefully, after tonight, they'd grow closer yet.

"It's going to be fine," Reed whispered to Simon while Andi was distracted by Cooper. "But if you're not sure, then we can change the plan."

"No." He gritted his teeth and shook his head. "I trust you."

Reed knocked his knee into Simon's. "Thank you."

"What are you two up to over there?" Andi asked, apparently not as enthralled as Simon had thought. Or maybe she was just an excellent multitasker. He could attest to her skill since he'd watched her in bed with the three of them on as many occasions as they could arrange in the past year.

"Can we tell her now?" Cooper asked, guaranteeing they'd have to. Andi wasn't the type of woman to let things slide. "She's going to love this."

Simon nodded when Reed and Cooper looked to him for one final reassurance that he was onboard. Cooper scooted his chair around so that the three of them sat shoulder to shoulder to shoulder directly across from Andi.

She beamed. "Well, that's a hell of a view, right there."

"We wanted to talk to you for a second." As usual, Reed acted as the spokesman for the guys. He was best at it.

Andi's smile dimmed some, making Simon wonder if he'd been right all along. He set down his fork on his empty plate and wrung his hands. When she glanced at his nervous gesture, she began to frown. Ah, shit. He was screwing things up already.

"It's nothing bad," Cooper promised her. "In fact, we wanted to surprise you."

"It's not my birthday." She tipped her head as she studied them. "Or a holiday. What's going on?"

"Technically, it kind of is." Reed smiled. "It's the anniversary of our graduation. And since we never got to celebrate properly, we were hoping you'd let us take you out. To Coeur."

There it was.

Simon tried not to wince. Coeur was the fancy-as-fuck French restaurant back in their college town where they'd planned to woo Andi originally, before they'd driven her to experiment at a random sex club, which had ended in disaster. Every time he so much as thought about her alone with that creeper, being drugged then assaulted…

He shuddered.

But Andi didn't.

Another point for Reed and Cooper. Andi flew from her chair and rushed around the table to them. Simon stood automatically when she approached, as did the other two guys. Good thing since she launched herself into their arms and let them squeeze them tight. Her feet kicked in the air as she squealed. The guys supported her petite frame easily, keeping her off the floor.

"Seriously?" She pulled back far enough to look at each of them. "We're finally going to eat there? Oh my God. I hope they still have that raspberry chocolate dessert thingy I was drooling over on the menu. I mean, not that I scoped it out last year or anything." She kissed Reed and Cooper on their cheeks, then squirmed until they put her down so she could approach Simon directly.

He couldn't help but grab her around the waist when she went onto her tiptoes to kiss his lips. While he'd always hated not being tall, he admitted now that it had some benefits. Whereas the other guys only scored a peck, he'd gotten a full-on smooch.

Which, of course, only made him crave another taste of Andi.

Who needed dessert when he had her?

"Will you wear the dress we bought you?" he wondered, imagining her svelte form draped in the purple silk. Better yet, he thought about what it would be like to unwrap her after they came home, showing off the expensive lingerie they'd ordered for her online.

He'd have to rein in Reed to keep him from tearing it off her, he'd bet.

"Hell yes. It's been hanging in the back of my closet, just waiting for the perfect occasion. When are we going?" she asked.

"It's a four hour drive, so...you have about two hours until we need to leave," Reed told her.

"Tonight?" Her gorgeous eyes widened, then she sprinted for the master bedroom and her en-suite bathroom, which she'd banned the guys from. It was her domain and they were glad to let her have it.

Although she'd never been a very girly girl, lately she'd accumulated a decent amount of stuff that looked like torture equipment to him and spent a few hours each week watching YouTube videos to figure out how to use it. At first, she'd concentrated on making her appearance more professional for her job, hoping people would take her more seriously if she looked mature. Lately he'd noticed her adding in some seductive flair for their benefit.

The three guys together didn't have as much shit as she did, which was a little hard to fathom since she was by far the best-looking of them and needed absolutely no help from lotions, potions, makeup, or whatever other gadgets she had stashed in there as far as he was concerned. Even so, he wasn't complaining. Whatever made her happy and more confident was fine with him. He approved of anything that made her feel as sexy as he already knew she was.

"I've got to get ready," she shouted as she rounded the corner, ducking out of sight.

"Don't forget the fuck-me heels," Reed called after her.

"Yes, sir," she called before she slammed the door and locked herself inside the bathroom. Although they'd only been joking—after all, he was pretty sure she didn't own anything other than sensible flats or running sneakers—Simon had to adjust his junk.

He would never have imagined it possible, but he was no longer afraid to admit that he got off on watching the kinky games Reed and Andi liked to play together. Having a front row seat to that much intensity and passion turned him on. Big time.

"You think she'll freak when she sees us in the tuxes we rented?" Cooper asked.

"Guaranteed." Reed grimaced. "It's not that I don't think you two were right about that, but I'm still not exactly looking forward to that portion of the evening."

"Me either." Simon wrinkled his nose as he considered giving up the soft sweatpants he was used to wearing, even in his position as a physical trainer for the Sabertooths, their city's football team.

"It won't hurt you two to look civilized for a single evening." Cooper stopped just short of rolling his eyes. Of course he did. After all, he loved dressing up. Had even signed himself up for a lifetime of daily suit-wearing by pursuing his law degree.

Simon couldn't imagine that being his goal in life. Then again, he wasn't Cooper and that was okay. Andi loved them all. At least he was pretty sure she felt as deeply about them as they did about her. Maybe tonight they would find out for sure.

REED BEGAN PACING the kitchen about an hour and a half after that. By two hours and ten minutes later, Simon was going to throat punch the guy if he didn't simmer down. "Relax. We have plenty of time."

"I don't want anything to ruin this." He turned to Simon and Cooper looking ruffled, completely out of character for him. Cooper stepped up and fixed Reed's bowtie, then straightened the lines of his formal jacket. If Reed couldn't hold it together, they'd do it for him, because that's what Andi deserved.

Simon should have realized it would be more than only himself on edge when they returned to their old stomping grounds. The night was more important than he'd imagined. Each of them needed to prove that they could do this. That they had survived and emerged victorious against all odds.

While Simon kept Reed from wearing out his shiny shoes, Cooper went and knocked on Andi's door. "Baby, are you almost finished? We need to leave soon and you're gorgeous exactly how you are. You don't need..."

"Go away, Cooper." Andi's voice was muffled.

"But Reed—"

"He can wait two seconds," she said, more firmly this time. "I want you guys to see me at the same time. Go back to the living room. I'll be right out, promise."

Simon straightened, his cock half-stiff imagining what she might look like. In reality, he knew he'd only be staring at her eyes, and maybe her smile, his two favorite features of hers. Though it seemed ridiculous, he had this reaction pretty much any time they were reunited.

He loved his job. He loved working with professional athletes and being part of a game that most people only ever got to watch from the other side of a TV. But it was a sacrifice being away from home, sometimes for weeks—or even months, during preseason training camps—at a time.

Tonight, though, they were all here. Together. And it was going to be epic.

Once Cooper had rejoined Simon and Reed, they didn't speak. The three of them held their breath, waiting for their girl.

She didn't disappoint.

Andi came down the hallway as if it were a catwalk, making the guys drool more than the thought of the five-star cuisine they were about to devour. If he wasn't mistaken, she'd highlighted her hair, adding hints of red, then did something to make it even smoother and shinier than usual. She'd also put a lot of effort into her makeup, emphasizing the features each of them liked best. Cooper ogled her lips, and Reed seemed transfixed by the cleavage she'd showcased in that smoking hot dress. Simon thought her eyes had never seemed to shine as bright as they did right then. Her legs looked much longer than he knew they were, thanks to a wicked set of heels.

Hot damn. Had Reed known she had them squirreled away?

When she caught sight of the three of them, standing together, dressed to the nines while Cooper held a bouquet of her favorite flowers, she nearly tripped. Her jaw dropped and she gaped at them.

"Careful, Andi. If you don't close your mouth, I'll be tempted to put something in it." Reed smirked as he teased her.

"Oh, fuck you." She laughed and gave him the finger. "You're ruining my entrance."

Uh oh. Simon knew she'd pay for that later. Not that Reed would ever lift a hand to harm her, but he sure as hell would be glad for some minor transgression to use as ammunition when he dragged out her sexual satisfaction much later in the evening.

It was going to be a wild night.

They all knew it.

But first, they'd pretend to be sophisticated.

3

———

Cooper couldn't pronounce half of what they'd eaten. That hadn't kept him from enjoying every tiny, fussy dish. Even better had been watching Andi's eyes light up at the colorful, edible arrangements. She'd licked fancy sauces off her fork, moaning softly as she savored the rich flavors that were presented to them throughout the multi-course meal, which lasted for hours.

Funny enough, he felt like he might be getting hungrier instead of more full as he, Reed, and Simon watched her eat. By the time they got to dessert, he wasn't sure how he was going to survive the drive home without having a nibble or two of Andi. If he thought it would work, he'd bribe the waiter into sending them off with a bottle of the gourmet chocolate syrup drizzled over their raspberry cake so that they could finish the night properly.

Four fucking hours in the car while his dick was as hard as one of the bazillion forks they'd used. He might need to jack off in the backseat to survive it.

Especially after he spent another five minutes watching Andi relish every last morsel on her gold-edged plate. He couldn't stop gawking at her lips.

She must have noticed because she spent extra time licking them clean of the smudges of chocolate in the corners before turning to him with a wicked grin.

Andi was teasing him? Oh no.

He couldn't take anymore and still act like he had manners.

"Are you ready to hit the road?" Cooper asked. They all knew what he really meant. It was a long drive and they were all horny as fuck. The sooner they left, the sooner they could be home in Andi's bed, enjoying the rest of their night.

"Would you mind walking me to the restroom first?" Andi asked, with a light touch on his forearm.

He winced, remembering a time when she would have gone on her own without a second thought. It thrilled him that she trusted him implicitly to protect her. Still, it bugged him that even now, in a swanky place like this, she didn't feel entirely secure.

"Of course I don't mind." He stood and held out his hand to her.

She took it, placing her fingers over his as Reed got up and pulled her chair out for her.

"Simon and I will go get the car and pull around front so she doesn't have to walk as far in those shoes." Reed scanned from Andi's face down the elegant little dress she wore, past her stockings to the killer heels she'd unearthed from the back of her closet.

She'd been holding out on them, damn.

Cooper extended his arm, sighing when she put her

hand in the crook of his elbow. He would have been lying if he hadn't admitted the pride he felt with a woman like her walking beside him. Not only because of the indecent things those shoes were doing to her already gorgeous legs, but also because of how brave, smart, and adventurous she was, too.

He was one of the three luckiest men on the face of the planet, and he wanted to make sure she knew it. When she ducked into the ladies' room, he drew his phone from his pocket and texted Reed and Simon.

Find us a hotel room. Somewhere nice. And close. Really close.

It would be a lot smarter to stay in the city instead of making the trek home. Now that Simon had a real job, Reed's company was getting off the ground, he'd taken on a paid internship at a law firm in Cunningham, and they were still saving money by living together, they could swing a few luxuries. A night with Andi in a posh hotel was well worth it.

Cooper leaned against the wall as he waited for a reply from the guys or for Andi to emerge. His ankles crossed, he tried not to get a boner as he thought about what could turn out to be one of the best nights of his life.

So he didn't recognize the person approaching until they said, "Hey there. Is that you, Cooper?"

"Mr. Schone!" He stood upright and stuck out his hand automatically, shaking his boss's. "What a coincidence, seeing you here."

Shit. They'd picked Coeur for a few reasons. Primarily because it had been the place they'd intended to treat Andi to last year, before everything had gone to shit. It hadn't hurt that it wasn't anywhere near their current neighborhood, though. After Andi's attack they'd been very careful about what they disclosed to others.

Their complex relationship wasn't something they talked openly about outside their house. It seemed better that way, for everyone. Coming here, they hadn't been too worried about being themselves or who would be watching if they got flirty. If anything, he figured they might bump into an old professor or maybe an underclassman waiting tables.

Not his damn boss.

At least the other guys were already out in the truck.

"Hey, hey. Don't make me feel old. It's just Marty out in the wild. And, yeah, I like to bring women here. Impress the panties off them, you know." Marty wiggled his brows.

Cooper probably should have been disgusted. Before he got too judgey, though, he figured he didn't have a lot of room to be throwing side-eye since some people would say that's what he, Reed, and Simon were doing with Andi.

It didn't feel quite the same, except—you know —guy talk.

"I assume, if you're hanging out here, that you're doing a little of the same." His boss grinned. "I always knew I liked you, kid."

Cooper tried not to let the food in his stomach sour. Something about the smirk his boss leveled at him grossed him out. Now, instead of wishing for Andi to hurry her ass up, he was hoping she took her time so he could get rid of Marty before he had to let the guy leer at her. He was exactly the kind of man who'd make her less comfortable going to the bathroom without a chaperone next time.

While Cooper ordinarily would have gone into the

men's room himself and continued their discussion there —or used typical man rules to shut Marty up while they pissed—there was no way he would be anywhere but right where Andi had left him when she came out of the bathroom, expecting him to be there for her.

So he gritted his teeth when Marty whipped his gaze to the opening door. His eyes widened and he shifted not-so-subtly, rearranging his package.

Cooper had to force his hands to stay relaxed instead of balling into fists. Thank God Reed wasn't there, or they'd probably be holding him back right then. Beating up a lawyer was an indulgence they couldn't afford yet. A hell of a lot more expensive than springing for a romantic evening, he was sure.

"Okay, I'm ready. Let's get out of here," Andi said as she strode to him and held out her hand. It tugged at his heart that she didn't even notice Marty, her gaze fixed on Cooper instead.

"Aren't you going to introduce me to this lovely lady first?" Marty spoke up a little too loud, startling Andi.

She covered it well, relaxing her shoulders and smoothing her features before turning to the other man with a smile. "I'm sorry. I didn't realize you two knew each other."

Yet, she stayed plastered to Cooper's side, waiting for him to elaborate.

"Andi, this is my boss. You've heard me talk about Mr. Schone. Marty, I mean." He kept hold of her, for some reason not wanting her to extend her hand or approach the other man. Jealousy? Maybe, but he didn't usually roll that way. After all, he happily shared Andi with his two best friends. "Marty, this is my girlfriend, Andi Miller."

That was the truth. Just not all of it.

No one needed to know more than that. In fact, they hadn't really defined their connection. Maybe they needed to talk about it. Things were serious after the past year they'd spent advancing their friendships into something far deeper.

Cooper loved Andi, and he knew Reed and Simon did, too.

Were they risking their relationship by not spelling it out?

"What a lucky bastard you are." Marty stepped close, but Cooper angled his shoulder so it wedged between his boss and Andi. "Why don't you have a picture of her on your desk? That certainly would brighten up the office."

"I'll be sure to bring one in." Cooper would definitely *not* be doing that, no matter what he said to placate the guy. He didn't need Marty peeping on Andi every time he stopped by to drop off a case file that needed to be researched. Hell fucking no. "Well, we should let you go so you don't keep your date waiting—wouldn't want to ruin your chances or anything."

Cooper couldn't care less if Marty didn't get any that night. In fact, he wondered if the woman he'd left out in the dining room wasn't counting her blessings, having a moment to herself to digest her food in peace.

"Good call." Marty grinned. "This is why you're at the top of your class. We're lucky to have you at the firm."

"Thank you," Cooper said, wondering if he was going to have to find somewhere else to work if things with Marty went south. He had to walk a fine line. He needed the credit from his apprenticeship so he could finish his master's degree and sit for the bar exam. Otherwise, the years of education and the student loans that came along with them, would be for nothing.

Andi saved the day. "It was nice to meet you. I hope you don't mind if I steal my boyfriend away now." She waved without waiting for a response, then began to stray farther down the hall, polite yet aloof. Was it because she didn't like meeting new people anymore, or because she didn't like Marty specifically? She had good instincts, even better ones since last year.

Cooper might have asked her except once they were out of earshot from Marty and ensconced in the car, Simon flashed Cooper a thumbs-up and Reed nodded. The guys were obviously onboard with Operation Hotel Romp.

"Change of plans, Andi," Reed said, drawing her attention before she could ask about what had obviously been an awkward situation back at the restaurant.

"Hmm?" She sank into the seat, relaxed now that she was surrounded by them and only them.

"Remember that place downtown that hosted your science department awards every year?" Simon blurted, obviously too excited to wait for Reed to fill Andi in.

"Yeah. I felt like an imposter even walking inside. Everything was so damn shiny and gorgeous. I can't believe some people live like that. What about it?" She tipped her head slightly to one side.

"Guess who has a reservation for the top-floor suite, complete with an in-room jetted tub and a couple of bottles of champagne?"

"Us?" She lifted her hand to her mouth, her freshly painted nails twinkling in the light from the street lamps. "You guys…"

"We're the best; we know." Simon grinned.

"You are." She blinked rapidly then. "Thank you. For tonight. For everything. For being with me."

"That's our pleasure, Andi. All ours." Reed reached over to squeeze her hand, then put the car in gear, driving them to where they would undoubtedly share one of the best nights of their lives.

4

Andi had no idea what she'd done to deserve not only one, but three extraordinary boyfriends who were thoughtful, attentive, easy to love, and incredible in bed. There was no doubt in her heart. She loved each of them and the complex relationship they'd built together. Not only did she care for them as friends and roommates, she was *in love* with Reed, Cooper, and Simon.

As much as that thought filled her with joy, it also terrified her.

Could this last? She'd given herself to them completely, committed to being *theirs*. How long could she keep all three happy? How could she be sure that she would always have the right to look at them and think... *yes, I'm theirs but they're also* mine.

Even the thought of losing them now—one or all—was devastating to her. She wanted to make sure that tonight she showed them just how much she needed each of them. Fortunately, it seemed easier to communicate that when they were in each other's arms—skin on skin on skin on skin.

Andi had no doubt that they would be naked moments after entering the grand room they'd rented. They might as well have booked a spot at a budget motel for all she'd know the difference. Right then, her criteria for an acceptable place to stay the night included two items only: It should be clean, and have a big bed. Nothing else mattered.

Of course, what was necessary and what was fun were two entirely different things.

Reed dealt with the valet while Simon and Cooper flanked her under the grand portico outside of the most luxurious hotel in the city. Each of them took one of her hands in theirs as they walked her through the gilded doors into the ornate lobby she'd admired on previous visits. Never had she imagined she might one day be a guest here, always feeling like an imposter as she hurried off to the ballroom that housed her science department's annual award ceremony.

In fact, she wished for a moment she had her hands back from her guys so she could adjust her dress and make sure there were no crumbs stuck to her or a smudge of chocolate left on her lips.

"Relax," Cooper told her. "You look great. Like you belong here."

"I belong with you guys." She told them with a soft smile, feeling overly emotional after the heaps of effort they'd gone to in order to make the evening so special.

"Yes, you do," Reed agreed as he came up behind them, then took the lead with the desk clerk, checking in and collecting the electronic keys to their room.

It was only a minute or two, thanks to impeccable

customer service, but enough time for Andi to look around and wonder how this could be her life. She couldn't wait to show the guys exactly how much she appreciated them. And desired them.

She shifted, rubbing her thighs together to squash some of the ache between them.

"Are your feet hurting?" Simon asked. "I can't imagine the strain those shoes must put on your anterior transverse arch. Want me to rub them when we're upstairs?"

Andi groaned. Simon gave the best massages. "I want your hands on me, yes. Absolutely."

He nodded. "Sure, no problem."

"But maybe in places that need attention more than my feet." She smiled sweetly, as if she hadn't propositioned him right there in the fancy lobby.

"Let's head for the elevators," Cooper said as he started tugging her in their direction. "Reed will catch up and let us know where to go."

They'd barely made it to the bank of elaborately etched doors when Reed strode to them, making short work of the distance with a powerful gait that did nothing to calm Andi down. "Trying to steal her away from me?" He stared at the three of them when he reached out blindly to smack the up button.

"Nah. Just getting a head start." Simon grinned. "It's like my dick knows we're about to get busy. I almost put on a very crude display for those distinguished guests around us. These tuxes don't hide much in the crotch region."

Of course, that meant Andi had to look.

"Oh my." She whipped her gaze forward, hoping no

one saw her peeping at the obvious bulges in her guys' pants.

"Don't say *dick*. We're trying to act like grownups, remember?" Reed chastised him.

"Besides, talking about how much amazing sex we're about to have is only making the problem worse." Cooper sounded like he was gritting his teeth.

Andi wondered exactly how long it would take the elevator to get to their floor. Probably not long enough for what she wanted to do to them inside it.

A pleasant *bing* sounded right before her men ushered her into the car. She stood between them, absorbing their heat and strength as it began to move. As if he could read her mind, Reed wrapped his arm around her from behind and pulled her against his rock-hard chest. He slipped his hand between her legs and cupped her mound.

She arched her hips, pressing into his hold. A moan slipped from between her lips and her head lolled onto his shoulder. Cooper and Simon whipped toward her at the sound. Cooper kissed her exposed neck and Simon's hands flew to her breasts.

With every floor they passed, she wondered if they would get busted.

The possibility only added to the thrill of having three men focused on arousing her. They had a lot of practice and were incredible at it. So she wasn't surprised when she felt an orgasm gathering after a few seconds at their mercy. Hell, they'd really been engaged in hours of foreplay already, if she was being honest.

Their touches gave the pressure that had been building within her since she prepared herself for them in her bathroom at home an outlet, one she fully embraced.

It would be the first of many tonight, she was sure of it. So she allowed herself to give in without a fight.

When Reed's thumb rubbed circles around her clit, she cried out. Cooper was there to swallow the sound. He kissed her deeply as she came. Thank God for Reed and Simon holding her up. Her legs became useless as rapture ripped through her in a powerful release that left her breathless.

"I've got you," Reed promised, swinging her into his arms as the elevator slowed and the doors opened on the top floor. "We're almost there."

The air left her in a huge rush. She went limp against Reed's chest, nuzzling her face against the crook of his neck. When she peeked over his shoulder, she saw Cooper and Simon flanking him, their faces flushed with awe and intense need of their own.

"That was hot," Cooper reassured her—he wasn't jealous she'd come when they were so obviously craving the same relief.

"Beautiful," Simon agreed.

"Next time you come, one of us is going to be inside you," Reed guaranteed. "I hope you're ready for a late night."

"Mmm." She snuggled into his hold as he stopped in front of a paneled double door.

"Get the key out of my pocket," he told Simon, who did.

Simon whistled as he let them inside. "Not that I was fishing around in there on purpose, but I'm pretty sure that wasn't a baseball bat I felt next to the keys. Are you going to be able to control yourself, big guy?"

Reed grimaced. "I'm counting on you and Cooper to tell me if I get too wild."

"How about you all let *me* worry about that?" Andi wriggled until Reed set her down, her heels sinking into the plush carpet. "Maybe I want something wild. I can handle you. All three of you. I don't want you to treat me like I'm fragile anymore. I want you."

She sank to her knees on the spot. "Get over here."

They approached, forming a semi-circle around her. Reed was in the middle, Simon on her left, and Cooper on her right. "First one to take their dick out gets my mouth."

Of course, Reed practically ripped his tux in his haste.

Andi licked her lips as her three guys bared themselves to her one by one. She leaned forward, true to her word, taking Reed deep into her mouth in one long swallow. He groaned and speared his hands into her hair, holding her face as he rocked against her.

Partially to steady herself, and partially because she didn't want the other two to go without, she reached a hand toward both Simon and Cooper, taking hold of their cocks as well.

They stiffened rapidly in her grasp, as if they were as hungry as she had been when walking over the threshold of Coeur. She might have been the one kneeling for them, but knowing she had the full attention of three amazing men flooded her with satisfaction. They had transformed her into the temptress she'd always longed to be instead of the inexperienced nerd she'd actually been throughout their college careers.

They had given her this power.

And she swore she'd never abuse it or use it for anything except bringing them as much pleasure as possible. Andi stroked Simon and Cooper while she toyed with Reed's shaft, bobbing over it while licking and sucking. She let her hands wander lower, cupping Simon and Cooper's balls, weighing them in her palms.

Even blindfolded, she'd be able to tell which guy was which. They reacted differently to her caresses. Cooper's sac tightened and he groaned while Simon pressed forward, eager for her to return to massaging his dick.

He might have been the most playful, but he packed some serious equipment. Thicker than the other two guys, it was good he preferred not to be as intense with her as Reed or even Cooper. Otherwise, she might be too sore to fuck each of them. And tonight, nothing less would be acceptable to her.

But she also wanted to ride them, or be ridden, for more than a few minutes. So she decided then and there that she was going to give them a bit of an appetizer, just like they'd done for her.

Andi leaned in and took Reed fully into her mouth, flexing around him. He growled her name in a warning she completely disregarded.

She wanted him to lose control. Wanted him to empty himself down her throat.

Cooper moaned. "Do it, Reed. She wants you to. Take the edge off so we can fuck her all night."

"Is that true?" he asked her.

She nodded, hoping he could tell the difference between that and the rest of her motions since she worked his cock as well as she knew how. Either he understood or he simply couldn't resist the increasing suction she applied to his shaft, because he went rock-hard, the veins on his shaft rubbing over her tongue a moment before he shouted her name.

His cock pulsed in her mouth before he began shooting, and didn't stop for longer than it took her to swallow his seed. She cleaned him off gently as he began to relax and his breath whooshed out of him in a rush.

He braced one hand on her shoulder as he withdrew from between her lips, then leaned down to kiss her. She loved that he didn't avoid communicating his thanks because he'd come in her mouth.

While they kissed, he rubbed her jaw. Thankfully, it wasn't uncomfortable. Truthfully, it hadn't taken much effort to get Reed off. This time.

Her eyes fluttered open when he retreated, just far enough that Cooper and Simon could fill the gap. "Who's next?" she asked as she grinned up at them.

"You don't have to—" Cooper started to reassure her, ever the gentleman.

"Simon it is, then." She winked to let him know she'd get to him, too.

Cooper cursed as she shifted her attention to Simon, who laughed. "Nice guys always finish last, don't you know?"

"I didn't think that was a literal saying," Cooper grumbled as Reed joined Simon, cracking up. "Oh, sure, asshole. Laugh all you want. You already came. Hard."

"Damn straight." Reed leaned up against a wall nearby, idly stroking himself. Andi peeked over. He hadn't gone completely soft. Good, she was already getting horny again herself.

She shifted her knees, which were plenty comfortable, nestled in the soft carpet.

Of course Reed noticed now that he had the use of some of his brain cells again. He circled around and crouched behind her. His hand brushed up the inside of her thigh even as she took Simon's cock between her lips.

"Careful, don't make her bite me," he teased Reed.

His concern was probably warranted. Andi tried to concentrate, but Reed's touch enflamed her. She directed her renewed enthusiasm at Simon's cock while never letting go of Cooper's. She sucked and jerked simultaneously, impressed with her increasing ability to handle more than one of them at a time even while Reed was doing whatever it was he was doing.

He'd cupped her mound from behind, then started tracing a line down her pussy with his middle finger, wedging her panties between her lips and rubbing circles around her clit. Damn him, she wanted to at least even the score before coming again.

She could already tell that wouldn't happen.

With three of them and only one of her, they were able to bring her nearly endless pleasure and were always able to give her as much as she craved. They took turns looking after her, making sure her needs were taken care of, while another was able to be more selfish.

Tonight was no exception.

Although Simon loved nothing more than watching her come. And so it made her job easier. She clung to his ass with one hand while her other still clutched Cooper's dick. She loved the heat and weight of Simon's shaft on her tongue, especially when Reed hit exactly the right spot. She sucked Simon furiously, glad for something to keep her from shrieking at the overwhelming pleasure Reed inflicted.

"Want you to come with me, Andi." Simon was serious about that. He brushed one thumb over her cheekbone, drawing her gaze sharply upward. When they stared at each other, she understood it was time.

Reed did something clever with his hand that triggered her orgasm. She moaned around Simon without ever looking away from him. He shuddered, then began to pump his come into her mouth. She swallowed it even as she came undone herself. Thank God Reed was there to hold her up again, keeping her in position for Simon and Cooper, who now fucked into her fist.

Simon slipped his cock from her mouth when he'd had enough, then mimicked Reed, leaning down to kiss her thoroughly before backing away.

"Would you like to lie on the bed?" Cooper asked her, willing as ever to forsake his pleasure for her comfort. "That looked like it wrung you dry."

"Mmm." She couldn't manage more than that. Aftershocks spread outward from her pussy, illuminating her entire body with sparkles from within.

When Cooper smiled and stroked her hair, as if he was about to lift her up and carry her to bed so she could recover in peace, she stopped him by tightening her grip on his cock.

"Not yet," she rasped before lunging toward him and taking his tip into her mouth. She fluttered her tongue over it, swiping the drop of precome pooled there before suckling the blunt head of his cock, exactly as he preferred.

"Oh shit." He stared up at the ceiling, his hands fisting at his sides.

"That's right," Reed cooed in her ear. "Show him how well you know what he likes. How perfect you are for him. For each of us. I bet you can make him come in the next sixty seconds if you try."

Game on. Andi focused her effort on Cooper alone, altering her technique to mash every one of his sexy buttons. He spread his legs as if he might fall over unless he steadied himself. Always one for fun and games, Simon began a countdown clock.

Andi had twenty-two seconds to spare when Cooper groaned and spilled himself into her mouth, flooding her with the proof that she could affect him—them—as deeply as they did her. She nearly purred in triumph when she sucked him dry.

"That was amazing, Andi," Reed whispered in her ear. "You're incredible."

Cooper could only nod for a moment. When he'd gathered himself, he reached down and drew her to her feet, hugging her tight as he lowered his mouth to hers. His kiss was sweet and gentle, exactly like he was most times. He sipped from her lips, then soothed her swollen mouth with light laps of his tongue before separating them slightly.

"Wow." She blinked at the three men standing around her, suddenly feeling the need for a few deep breaths. They did that to her sometimes. Overloaded her senses with masculinity and pure sex appeal.

Andi turned away, resting her forehead against the floor-to-ceiling window she'd hardly noticed on the way in. It was cool and refreshing against her flushed skin. Now that she could think straight again, she glanced around the enormous suite in the reflection, taking in the opulent fabrics and the expanse of glass that allowed them to look out over an entire city's worth of lights, twinkling just for them. Or at least it seemed like it.

"This view is fantastic." She put her palms on the window-wall and surveyed the skyline. She'd never seen the city quite this way before. Everything looked different now that she was on top of the world. And it had everything to do with the three men behind her.

She looked over her shoulder at them and smiled. The night had only begun. It held so much potential, she didn't know where to go from here. Every direction seemed promising.

"Yes. Yes, it is," Cooper said as he stared directly at her.

"This way isn't so bad either." She turned and faced the guys, who stood in a line before her. Damn, the three of them in somewhat-disheveled tuxedos nearly stopped her heart. Sure, she loved the way they looked when they were hanging around the house in well-worn jeans or sweats and holey T-shirts from their alma mater, but this...

Andi fanned her face. "Is it hot in here?"

"Not as hot as it's about to be." Simon winked at her.

5

"Oh, really?" she couldn't help teasing them. "Are you planning to start a fire? I mean, I know Cooper was a proper Eagle Scout and all, but that might be a little much in a place like this."

"Well, there is an actual fireplace next to the Jacuzzi in the corner over there." Reed gestured with his chin. She would have thought he was shitting her except, now that he mentioned it, the sleek marble façade in that section of the room made more sense.

"Would you like to try that out?" Simon asked.

"Later." They already had her in danger of combusting if they didn't act on the tension mounting between them again. Damn.

The guys had the last laugh when the three of them began removing their bowties then unbuttoning their shirts. Holy shit. She leaned back against the window, glad for the low cut of her skimpy dress, which allowed the cool air rolling off the glass to help combat the blast of steaming sexiness that damn near scorched her front.

"What's the matter, Andi?" Reed asked. "Not joking anymore?"

"Nope." She was very serious all of a sudden. Because although they'd taken the edge off her desire, that didn't mean it was permanently dulled. Already she shifted, pressing her thighs together as she imagined how they were likely to spend the rest of the evening.

"You ready to get undressed?" Reed wondered. It was a rhetorical question, really.

Andi nodded anyway.

The guys stalked closer, surrounding her in a way that could have frightened her yet only made her feel secure instead.

Simon dropped to his knees to remove her shoes while Cooper walked her dress up her body then over her head. In the meantime, Reed held her hands, steadying her, as their roommates stripped her down to her lingerie in seconds flat.

They left her standing there in deep plum lace as they paused to admire her.

"Damn, girl." Simon reached out and drew his finger along the boning of the teddy that highlighted the best aspects of her figure and camouflaged the parts she didn't love as much. "I didn't think you could look more beautiful than you did in that dress."

"Get it off her," Reed practically snarled at Cooper.

"You don't like it?" She tried not to let Reed's dismissiveness hurt her feelings. Andi supposed she couldn't please all three of them all of the time.

Cooper laughed. "No, he likes it too much."

Even Simon rolled his eyes at her. "More like he's going to shred it trying to get to you since it turns him on so much. And he wants to see you in it again. Often."

Was that true? Andi looked up at Reed as Cooper began undoing the series of hooks that ran down the center.

Reed's jaw was clenched and his nostrils flared. Oh. Yup. He was a fan after all.

Andi smiled, slowly and surely. Her confidence rushed back. "In that case…why don't you show me how much?"

Cooper finished peeling the garment from her. Simon had done the same for her stockings, unhooking them and rolling them down her legs not a moment too soon.

Reed rushed her, grabbing her around the waist and tossing her over his shoulder as he marched to the bed. He dropped her on the elaborate four-poster that was even more massive than the one that took up an entire wall of her bedroom in their apartment.

What did two people do when they slept in a monster like this? Huddle in the middle or sleep with a mile of blankets between them?

Fortunately, she didn't have to find out.

In the few moments it took her to speculate about the bed, the guys stripped off their tux pants, socks, and underwear. The moment they were naked, she needed to touch them.

Andi held her arms up and open, and Simon flew into them. He rubbed his nose against hers and flashed one of his gorgeous smiles before kissing her stupid. She ran her hands over the muscles in his back and lower, to his ass. Reed took up a spot on the opposite side of her and snuck his hand between their torsos to fondle her breasts. He loved to play with them. Fortunately, he was also skilled at it.

Fun for him enhanced her pleasure. Everyone was happy.

As she found out again when Cooper joined them, separating her feet to make room for his body between her thighs. He crawled upward, licking and nipping a path from her knee straight to her pussy.

Andi would have called out his name, but Simon swallowed her cry. He devoured her moans and fed off her delight.

Right when she got serious about focusing on the sensations gathering within her, Reed pinched her pebbled nipples. He twisted them, adding a sharpness to the liquid desire Cooper and Simon had inspired.

It was the perfect blend of passions.

And when Cooper pressed two fingers inside her, giving her something to hold within her, she knew she wasn't going to last long enough for them to finish their foreplay.

Or was that fourplay? She might have laughed at her own dumb joke if Cooper hadn't chosen that exact moment to curl his fingers inside her and press upward, rubbing against her pubic bone. He knew, damn him, that she couldn't resist when he touched her there.

Especially not when Reed and Simon were doing their best to make her shatter, too.

Cooper warned the guys, "She's about to come again."

Simon smiled into her eyes and flicked his tongue over hers while Reed increased the pressure of his fingers and thumbs, rolling her nipples between them. Cooper ensured she did as he'd promised she would by leaning in to lick her clit while he continued his skilled manipulation of her flesh from the inside out.

She couldn't have stopped her climax if she'd wanted to.

And she definitely didn't want to.

It rolled through her, from her toes to the tips of her fingers, infusing her with warm tingles that would have satisfied a less greedy woman. Or maybe one who hadn't been spoiled this past year.

The crest only made Andi hungry for more. Before her body had finished wringing Cooper's fingers, she snaked her hand past Simon and Reed to grab his hair. With a tug, she let him know what she wanted.

Him. Higher up. His cock buried inside her.

Enough of this almost-sex shit. She had three willing men with hard cocks at her disposal, and she intended to use them well.

"You want him to fuck you?" Reed asked.

Andi would have nodded, but Simon was still there, kissing the shit out of her.

Reed nudged Simon's shoulder, letting her speak. "What do you want, Andi? Tell us and we'll give it to you."

"I want Cooper to put his dick in me while I suck Simon's cock, and you..." Andi lost her courage for a moment. She might be wanton, but she was still getting used to being a seductress. Sometimes she reverted to Andi the nerd and recent college graduate. Especially when it came to requesting something a little more...unconventional.

You know, like sex with three guys at once, she teased herself.

Because that's precisely what she craved.

"Tell me what you're asking for." Reed narrowed his eyes at her. "Make sure I understand so I can make your wishes come true."

"I want all three of you inside me at the same time," she blurted.

"If Cooper's got your pussy, and Simon's in your

mouth…" Reed increased his grip on her breast subconsciously. "Where do you want me?"

The three guys seemed to hold their breath as they waited for her to admit it.

"In my ass. Please." She shifted restlessly on the mattress. Would he be up for it?

Reed growled. "Hell yes. You're going to love this. I'll make sure you do."

Of course he would.

He leapt into action. "Cooper, get inside her. Distract her while I get her ready. Simon, you watch her carefully while she's sucking you. If you see even the slightest wince or a flicker of fear in her eyes, I want to know about it."

Simon nodded while Cooper simply did as he was told. Cooper took his cock in hand and came closer, until he fed her pussy inch after inch of his erection.

Andi moaned and slapped her palms on the comforter. "Yes!"

"Good. Keep going. I'll be right back." Reed rushed from the bed. Some sliver of Andi's mind wondered where he'd gone. Most was occupied with absorbing Cooper's strokes as he fit himself to her and the pressure of Simon's cock against her lips.

She smiled up at him, and licked the head of it.

He speared his fingers into her hair then tipped her face toward him and eased himself inside her parted lips. She sucked gently at first, as he liked best, then began to swirl the flat of her tongue over the underside of his shaft.

"Damn, Andi. That feels so good," he praised her as she lost herself in blowing him while Cooper began to move within her. She couldn't imagine sex getting any better than that.

Until it did.

Reed returned with a triumphant shout. "Look what I found!"

Andi couldn't see, so he filled her in along with the guys. "They had all sorts of fancy shit in the bathroom, including this organic coconut oil. Google says this will work nicely."

Work? Andi wondered if he was planning to give himself a facial while they were fucking until he barked at Cooper, "Roll over. Let her be on top so I can prep her with this."

Oh, right. Lube.

Thank God he was thinking straight, because she was lost to pleasure and the anticipation of being stuffed full of the three men she loved more than anything. Any last ability she had to form coherent thoughts vanished when Cooper wrapped her in a bear hug, then rolled, stealing Simon's cock from her in the process.

She whimpered and reached out with her opposite hand to reclaim him, sighing as he guided her mouth back to his shaft. Andi paused to nuzzle his balls and draw them into her mouth. His groan echoed around the room.

Her body rocked, pushing Cooper deeper inside her. She savored the taste of Simon's skin and his precome when she traveled upward, the head of his cock popping between the ring she made of her lips, which rolled over her teeth to make sure she didn't gouge him with them.

Cooper's hands cupped her hips, guiding her and helping her to ride him steadily despite the distraction of Simon in her mouth and Reed's palms, which began to knead her ass. She shivered when his finger trailed between her cheeks only to return, pressing deeper on his next pass.

That's when she realized he was melting the coconut

oil, warming it in his hands before spreading it across her skin. Her ass. Her muscles clenched when his finger rubbed harder, pressing the barest bit inside her tight hole.

Cooper groaned, and Simon whispered, "Careful, Andi."

Focusing on keeping her jaw loose so she didn't hurt him prevented her from reflexively tensing and making Reed's initial penetrations painful. She moaned as he breached her. With his fingers inside her, beginning to pump slowly—so slowly—she trembled.

This was exactly where she wanted to spend the rest of her life. Between them. Possessed by the three most amazing men she'd ever met.

"Damn, that looks so sexy," Simon murmured to no one in particular. He put his hand on his chest, his thumb strumming his own nipple idly as he began to thrust his cock into her mouth, fucking her as he watched Cooper and Reed doing the same.

Cooper groaned beneath her. "I wish I could see."

"Does that mean you want to trade places?" Simon asked.

"Nah, I'm good. This is good. Fucking incredible." Cooper pumped upward from beneath her, filling her more fully on that stroke. Her pussy undulated, trying to pull him even deeper, though it wasn't possible. She held him completely within her. His momentum drove her backward, further onto Reed's fingers.

"I can feel him fucking you. You know that, right?" Reed groaned. "I bet that feels so good. It's going to be even better when I'm doing it, too. Working with him to make you scream. You want that?"

"Mmmm," she moaned around Simon's dick. The

sound allowed him to press deeper into her throat. Andi swallowed around him, hoping he didn't feel left out.

"Good. Because this is my favorite," Simon told Cooper, resuming their banter and reassuring Andi in the process. "She gives the most amazing blowjobs. The best of my life."

Andi did her best to top that then. She licked, suckled, and hummed around him while Cooper kept up his steady pace and Reed began to stretch her wide with his fingers. It wasn't too long before he declared, "She's ready."

And Andi was.

So ready.

She cried out when he took his hand away, but didn't have to wait long before he replaced it with his cock. The fact that it slipped off the mark a few times made her sure he'd slathered himself with the natural lubricant.

When he finally plunged a few inches inside, his cock bumping into Cooper's, separated by only a thin barrier within her body, she shuddered.

"Does that hurt?" Simon asked her, withdrawing his cock from her mouth, instantly bringing Reed and Cooper to a stop as they waited for her response.

"No. Feels good. Fuck me. Please." Overwhelming? Yes. Painful? Hell no.

Andi craned her neck toward Simon, wanting his heat and weight back on her tongue as Reed and Cooper impaled her. They alternated driving in deeper as the other retreated, rubbing against each other's lengths even as they fucked her.

Rapture spiraled higher within her, making her tense and hover on the precipice of falling into the most powerful orgasm of her life. She resisted, wanting the pleasure to last forever. Until through some unspoken agreement, Reed and Cooper changed their approach.

They began to fill her simultaneously. Moving together to bring her as much ecstasy as possible. Simon cheered them on. "Look how flushed she is, how much her spine is arching. She's sucking me harder, too. You're going to make her come."

Andi tried to shake her head, as best she could with Simon's cock in her mouth.

"Hang on. I think she wants us to come with her," he told the other two guys.

Andi opened her eyes and stared up at him, nodding as she swallowed around him.

"Yes. That's what she wants." He spoke for her, becoming her voice when she had none. He stroked her hair, brushed his thumb across her lips, which were stretched around him. "Damn. I want that, too, Andi. I'm not going to last much longer anyway."

"Me either," Cooper groaned from beneath her. He fucked faster now, Reed matching him stroke for stroke. "Are you ready, Reed?"

"I've always been ready for this." He smacked Andi's ass hard, heating her flesh even as he rode her. "Go ahead, Andi. Come for us. We'll fall with you."

Reed used his other hand to rub down the length of her back. A simple touch. A possessive one. It made her arch against Cooper, rubbing her clit on the muscle above his dick. And that's all it took.

She exploded between them.

Her pussy and ass pulsed rhythmically around Cooper and Reed, making each of them groan and curse. She felt them swell within her a moment before they began to shoot. Simon joined them, flooding her mouth even as the other two guys overflowed her body with the proof of their pleasure.

Together, the four of them orgasmed. When it seemed one of them was winding down, another would groan or thrust in a reflexive aftershock that would prolong her euphoria. Andi had never climaxed so hard or so thoroughly in her life. She was still quaking when Reed pulled out, then Simon, then Cooper.

It was too much effort to open her eyelids, so she lay there, limp and floating as the guys took care of her. They cleaned her up, tipped a flute of champagne to her lips so she could sip from it, then arranged her beneath the covers, nestled between them.

She wasn't sure who held her or who it was behind her or who she was burrowing her cheek against. It didn't matter. They were all part of one whole. A satisfied, wrecked ball of love and spent lust.

Blissfully wrapped in her three men, Andi let them shower her with affection and soft praise as she drifted into a sound sleep, certain that when she was old and thought back on a lifetime of incredible nights spent with her lovers, this would have to be the best of them all.

6

Andi struggled to emerge from the haze of a deep slumber. Great sex was better than sleeping pills. She had no idea how long she'd been out. The light was odd and hazy. Or maybe that was her eyes. She scrubbed them with her fists. No luck. That same weird glow permeated the room.

She reached out on either side of her, expecting to find at least a man or two sharing the bed. Except there wasn't anyone there. The sheets were crumpled. The pillows weren't. Hadn't Cooper, Reed, or Simon slept with her after their wild night?

Something was wrong.

Andi clutched the sheet to her chest as she sat up, her hair a wild tangle around her face. "Guys?"

No one answered her.

She bolted from bed and threw on a robe, cinching it around her waist as she began to poke around the other rooms of the suite. There wasn't anyone sleeping in those beds either. No one in the bathroom. No clothes on the floor.

What the fuck?

Andi raced toward the entryway, where she caught up to her roommates, who were putting on their jackets and lacing up their shoes. Were they leaving her?

"What's going on?" she asked, hoping there was some other explanation for what was happening. Maybe they'd been going out to grab a late-night snack or to catch the highlights of some sportsball thing in the hotel bar, or maybe they had to move the car. But would they all go to take care of something like that and leave her alone?

No. This was something worse. Much worse.

"I'm sorry. I thought I could do this, but..." Cooper shrugged, then turned away, avoiding meeting her wounded stare.

"What did I do?" she asked.

"It's just too hard to love someone and know they're not really mine. To have to share like this," Simon added.

Reed simply nodded, his arms crossed over his chest in the manner she'd come to recognize. His mind was made up. Nothing she would say could change it now.

They *were* leaving her. Giving up on making this work.

How could they after last night? After all the things their careful planning had said to her even if the words remained unspoken aloud?

She didn't care if it made her pathetic. Andi begged for them to stay as her heart tore into tiny pieces. "We can figure this out. Please don't go!"

Instead of coming closer, they filed through the door and out of her life.

"Simon, Cooper, no! Reed!" she screamed as he too turned and left the room.

Andi thought she would die from the pain of losing them. Each of them, all at once. Except her vision faded and the scene in front of her morphed into the one she'd expected on waking. Reed hovered over her, his mouth twisted into a grim frown when she thrashed in his hold, still in the clutches of her nasty dream.

Her pulse hammered through her chest, which felt like it might explode. Her hands were locked into fists, and her feet thrashed against the sheets. Until she realized her men were still there. They hadn't left.

Andi went limp, the fight draining out of her. "Reed?"

"Yes, it's me. I'm right here." He hugged her tight, rocking her gently back and forth. "You were having a nightmare. You're here with us. Safe."

Cooper and Simon looked at her, their brows drawn and their mouths pinched tight. Worried. For her. Right away she knew what they had assumed—that she was reliving her attack in her sleep as she had those first few months afterward—but the relief that wrapped around her like a security blanket, knowing they were still there with her, prevented her from correcting them right away. "Thank God you're here."

She clutched Reed to her, squeezing him with arms she was surprised to see were shaking. Cooper rubbed her back with one broad hand from where he lay on her left side and Simon snuggled up close on her right.

"I'm sorry. I didn't think about how coming here might bring back bad memories." Reed scrunched his eyes closed. "I should have guessed that staying only a few blocks away from Flesh might remind you of the attack."

"That's not what happened." She calmed herself—and him, too—by running her fingers through his hair. "I mean, I was dreaming. Though not about that night."

"Then what had you so scared?" Cooper asked quietly.

"I dreamt that this was too much...or maybe not

enough...for you guys." She hated the tears that spilled down her cheeks as she shared her biggest fear. Sometime in the past year the things she was afraid of most had changed. Sure, she was wiser now and more cautious when it came to trusting strangers or putting herself in a position where she could be at risk.

But losing the guys...that possibility scared her far more than the thought of someone hurting her physically. One she knew she could survive, because she already had. The other... Well, she didn't want to find out if she could live without them.

"What?" Simon looked at her as if she was speaking in a foreign language.

"You decided you needed someone who was yours. For just you. That you didn't want to share me anymore." She sniffled, her stomach cramping saying the words out loud. Did that make her selfish? She knew it did.

"Don't take this the wrong way, Andi." Reed backed off far enough that he could meet her gaze directly. "But what we have...it's not *only* about you."

Strangely, that did make her feel better. "It's not?"

"Nah." Cooper smiled softly. "I've gotten used to having these guys around, too. They're my best friends. An important part of my life. Just like you."

"What we have, while it might be weird to others, works for us. And that's all that matters," Simon reminded her gently. "We're not going anywhere. You can count on us, promise."

She nodded shallowly, able to draw a deep breath for the first time since she'd roused. "Sorry. It was just a dream."

Reed gave her a look like he might argue. Cooper stopped him with a shake of his head as if he knew that now wasn't the right time to press her. She appreciated his awareness that, still ragged inside, the slimy coating of fear in her gut hadn't entirely vanished yet.

Maybe it never would go away completely.

Andi bit her lower lip as she asked, "What time is it anyway?"

Now that she was calmer, she could tell it was closer to morning than midnight. Birds chirped and there was a faint glow—a normal one, unlike the kind in her dream—on the horizon.

"About five-thirty." Cooper confirmed her suspicions. On a regular day they'd probably be getting up soon. Simon and Reed often went for a run around this time before getting ready for their days. Sometimes she and Cooper stayed in and snuggled, or fucked, then made breakfast so they could eat together before going their separate ways—him to school, her to the lab. Other times Simon was on the road with the team or Reed was gone on business trips.

But they spent the time together when they could.

Today was no different.

It was early, but not the middle of the night. She was up. So she might as well make the most of it. "Why don't we order room service and watch the sunrise from the Jacuzzi?"

"Damn, Andi. That does sound like a good way to start the day." Simon was already lunging for the menu beside the phone on the nightstand. "The warm water and pressure will also help work out any kinks left from last night's...*ahem*...activities."

When Reed finally loosened his hold and laid her down on the bed, she stretched, wincing a little at the tenderness in her muscles and joints. "Yeah, I could use a good soak."

"You? I'm pretty sure he's talking about us." Cooper laughed.

Reed climbed from bed then, exaggerating as he walked like the Tin Man, hunched over and clasping his back. "I'm getting too old for this."

"You're twenty-two, asshole." Simon threw a pillow at Reed, hitting him in the back of the head.

Andi couldn't help but grin at their antics. Every moment that passed helped erase her lingering terror and the blackness of her nightmare from her mind. How could she dwell on the darkness when rose-gold light spilled over the horizon, limning the skyline?

"Hurry, it's starting." Andi crossed to the whirlpool and climbed inside, settling herself so that she had a prime view. Simon switched on the faucets, which filled the tub remarkably quickly with steamy water.

Andi sighed and let herself melt against the wall of the contoured tub for several minutes.

Reed was returning from the bathroom when a knock came at the door. He detoured to claim their breakfast. His booming thanks rang through the suite before he reappeared with an entire cart laden with fancy silver-domed dishes and a crystal pitcher of OJ that would be awesome mixed with a hint of their leftover champagne from the night before.

"Holy shit. What did you order?" Cooper asked Simon.

He shrugged. "No idea. When I said I'd like breakfast, they said they'd send a selection right up. I guess it's a perk of the honeymoon suite."

The guys didn't say much then. As much as last night's dinner had been for her, this was their style of feast. They piled their plates high, then climbed in beside her. Heaps of bacon, pancakes, and eggs disappeared into their mouths. Andi grinned as she recalled the energy they'd burned the night before. They deserved a few extra helpings.

She settled on a selection of fruit and a donut or two. Hey, she'd earned them—sprinkles and all.

Simon leaned over when she'd finished and licked the icing from her fingers. "Mmm."

Andi giggled and kicked her feet in the flow of water in the Jacuzzi.

"That's better." Reed nodded. "It kills me when you're scared or upset."

She stiffened some, sure the temporary reprieve they'd granted her was over. In the bright light of day, they were going to have to talk more about her fears.

"I know you said this nightmare was different, but we're obviously at a crossroads." Cooper frowned, choosing his words carefully, unlike Simon, who would have blurted his feelings out, or Reed, who would rather fuck them out. "Do you think it would help to see the therapist again? You know any of us—all of us, if you want —would be glad to go with you if you think talking to someone would help."

Andi had gone to a few sessions after moving to Cunningham, but hadn't kept up with her appointments after she'd felt secure in her new home. Once the guys had finally gotten their act together and moved in with her, she'd felt safe again.

It was the thought of being without them that terrified her now.

"We could do that, sure. It doesn't hurt to have help working through the kinks in a relationship and, let's face it, ours is bound to have more pitfalls than most. I think what's bugging me is realizing that for the past year, I've been hiding. Not giving you guys the acknowledgement I should to the rest of the world. I'm the luckiest woman alive, and no one knows it." Andi sat up, leaning her head on Reed's shoulder while she clasped Cooper's hand and hooked her leg over Simon's. "I don't want to do that anymore. I want to go places with you guys. Do more things like we did this weekend. Make sure we're fully embracing our choice to be together."

"I'm onboard with that." Cooper nodded.

"Me, too," Simon said.

"I'll tell anyone who listens how fortunate I am to have you and two of the best friends a guy could have." Reed stared at each of them. "I'm not afraid to show the world what we share. Nothing someone else says will change how I feel about what we've got going, I promise you that."

Andi sighed, the warmth of the water—or maybe their affection—seeping into her bones. It felt like a major step in the right direction.

"In that case, are you guys finally going to let me hook you up with tickets to one of the Sabertooths' games? We're playing at home next Friday. Want to come?" Simon leaned in, his eyes open wide.

Andi realized then that her timidity had cost them all. It was her turn to support each of them the way they'd done for her. "Of course I'd love to see your work in action. What do you say, guys? Be my dates?"

Reed and Cooper high-fived over her head, then started taking bets on which one of them could eat the most hot dogs.

Andi grinned even as the warmth penetrating her

moved farther south. "That sounds fantastic, guys. Until then, let's make the most of the rest of our time here."

"What she means is...time for tub sex." Simon waggled his eyebrows.

Andi would have laughed. Before she could, Cooper had claimed her mouth and Reed straddled her thighs, standing so he could cup her breasts and press the tip of his already hard cock between them. Apparently she wasn't the only one who liked the idea of going public with their relationship.

Simon slid beneath her so that she was sitting in his lap, her back to his chest, and his hard-on nestled between her thighs.

It didn't take long before they'd wiped every last trace of worry from her brain and replaced it with undying ecstasy.

7

"Yo. There's a fine young woman out in the hall, looking for you." One of Simon's star athletes smacked him on the ass as he jogged past in the warm-up area. "Better hurry up and see what she wants before the rest of the guys notice her and try to give her a tour of the locker room."

Simon finished wrapping an ankle quickly but efficiently before practically sprinting over to the entrance separating the staff area from the general stadium space. He flashed his badge to the security guard before surrounding Andi in a bear hug. He kissed her right out in the open, where anyone could see.

Fuck that. He hoped his colleagues finally realized how lucky he really was and why he didn't often take them up on their offer to hang out at sports bars after practice or at the end of game days. He lifted his chin at Reed before bumping the other guy's fist, still without letting go of Andi.

Simon loved that she had popped in for a closer look at his work. It was a treat that she, Cooper, and Reed had been able to make it. It felt so weird keeping them separate from parts of his life. Unnatural, despite what anyone else might say about their arrangement.

"I know you're busy—" She glanced over her shoulder at Reed like she might turn around and leave. Simon loosened the hold of his arm, which was slung over her shoulder, trying not to squish her in his enthusiasm.

"Nah. You have great timing." He wasn't about to let her flee. "Coach rounded up the players for the pre-game briefing. I've got about twenty minutes before they're going to need me again. Want a tour?"

"Sure." She smiled then, placing her hand in his.

Simon glanced over at the security guard on duty. It wasn't one of the guys he'd gotten to know over the past year. "Hey man, I don't suppose you'd let me bring in two guests for a couple minutes?"

"Sorry. No can do." The guard crossed his arms and shook his head. "One's the limit."

Simon didn't blame him for sticking to the stadium policy. It kept him...and Andi...protected after all. Hopefully Reed would understand.

"Go ahead." Reed waved his hands at them, taking a step back before Simon could even explain the rules. "Cooper is in line for some junk food. And you've only got a little while to spare. I'll go next time."

"You're sure?" Simon asked.

"Yeah. Of course." Reed smiled. "Have fun, kids. I'll wait right over here for you, Andi."

"Thanks." She blew him a kiss, then gave Simon her full attention.

He stood a little taller, his chest puffed out as he led her through the guts of the stadium and pointed out all the stuff that was part of his routine. Seeing the facilities through her eyes, for the first time, he felt pretty damn good about himself and how far he'd come in his first real job after college. Between that, living somewhere other than his parents' basement, and being in his first meaningful relationship—if an unusual one—he might just be making something of his life.

Andi looked up at him, her eyes wide as she surveyed the sports medicine bay. "It's really cool to picture you here, doing what you're best at. It's a little weird, too, to see you being so serious."

"When it comes to the athletes' health, yeah, I've got to be all boring and shit. Any other time...not so much." He laughed as he showed her his various treatment stations, careful to avoid the entrance to the locker room.

Instead, he detoured to a thick, blue-painted steel door with no windows.

No one else would give a shit about this particular spot. It only mattered to him. As the low man on the totem pole, he was responsible for reordering supplies and keeping the rest of the medical staff fully stocked with whatever they required.

He plucked a key hanging from a lanyard around his neck off his chest and leaned down to fit it into the lock. "This spot is pretty much my domain. We stash our materials in here. I wouldn't ordinarily bother showing you this, but maybe it'll interest you because it's stuff we get from Reed now that his company won the bid for the contract."

When he ushered Andi inside, he pivoted on the heels of his sneakers and flipped the lock. The noise made her jump. Then she whirled around and realized it was only him and her inside. Simon waggled his brows to erase any lingering distress from her features. "I'm the only person with a key."

She tapped the screen of her phone and checked the time. "Ten minutes until you need to be back out there?"

He nodded. "Give or take."

"I can work with that, and I'd really, really like to give for once." She stepped closer, into his open arms, and wound her arms around his neck. "I feel like I take too much."

"Not from me," he promised a moment before she sealed her lips over his.

It still blew his mind, how Andi fit him so perfectly even though he'd seen how she meshed as seamlessly with Reed and Cooper, who were nothing at all like him. She settled into his embrace, their chests mashed together as he teased her lips with the tip of his tongue. She had to be able to feel how much he wanted her.

His cock was trapped between them, hard just from having her nearby.

Simon ran his hands down her back then over her tight ass to the tops of her thighs. He slid them up again, this time under her skirt. When his fingers could reach the waistband of her panties, he nudged them down until they tangled around her thighs.

Only then did he stop kissing her, and only long enough to kneel so he could guide the scrap of satin down her legs, over her shoes, then help her step out of it.

"I'm glad you wore this skirt." He winked up at her.

"Me, too." She smiled as she squeezed his shoulder. "Maybe I was hoping we'd have a chance to make my first visit a memorable one."

"I think you're definitely going to do that, Andi." He didn't want to waste another second of the gift she so obviously intended to give him. The only thing that could have made it better was if Cooper and Reed had joined her.

He was honest enough with himself to admit that he enjoyed their time alone, too. They didn't have any hard and fast rules between them about when they could be together and who had to be there...or not. They did whatever came naturally.

Right now, every instinct he possessed was screaming for him to reward Andi for being so brave and so open. He squatted as he lifted her, pressing her shoulders against the door. She gasped as her back slid along the smooth, cold metal until her knees hooked over his shoulders. When he straightened, her pussy was at mouth-level, exactly where he wanted it.

"Make sure you keep leaning back, okay?" He squeezed her ass to help her concentrate on his words instead of the heat and vibration from his question, which she had to be able to feel on her core.

"Uh huh." She nodded.

"And try not to scream." He grinned up at her for a moment before he craned his neck enough to bury his face between her legs. Immediately the sweet taste he associated with Andi burst over his tongue.

She squeaked, then lifted her hand over her mouth, clasping it there as if to hold any stray sounds inside. It was a shame he couldn't tell her to shout her pleasure to the rooftop. He did happen to like his job, though, and he'd like to keep it. Not that he'd be the first guy busted having sex around here. The athletes, their egos, and the women who threw themselves at their feet meant nothing would shock management anymore.

Simon clutched Andi's ass, holding her in position as

he licked every bit of her damp flesh. She tucked the tops of her feet beneath his arms and against his torso, locking herself into place as she rode his face.

He used his tongue to trace around her clit, then lower, making the same circuit over and over, relentlessly. When she shivered in his hold, he raised his chin just enough that he could close his lips over her now hard clit, then suckled lightly, just like she liked it.

Andi shuddered. She dropped her free hand to the top of his head and clutched his hair hard enough to make his dick stand up and take notice. He couldn't tell if she was trying to hold on—not that she had to worry, he wasn't about to let her fall—or if she was trying to shove his head closer to her pussy.

Either way, he liked it.

He only regretted that from this angle, he couldn't slide his fingers deep inside her so that he could feel the muscles wrapped in soft, wet flesh hugging his hand as he brought her closer to orgasm. It was his business to know his way around the human body, and he applied every bit of that knowledge to thrill her.

Therefore, he wasn't surprised when he only got in a few more pulses of his mouth around her clit before she came. Andi bucked, making him chase her sweet pussy with every rock of her hips.

Simon devoured the arousal turning his mouth and chin slick. And when she went slack, he was quick to lower her gently until she was half-standing, half-leaning on him. Her skirt fell neatly into place.

He should have known that she wouldn't let him have all the fun.

After a few moments and ragged breaths, Andi tucked her fingers in the elastic waist of his track pants, then yanked them to his knees along with his underwear. He couldn't believe this was actually about to happen.

Thank God there were no cameras in the medical suite for the players' protection.

She licked her lips as she watched his cock bobbing stiffly in her general direction.

"Oh no." He covered his cock with his fist in case she got any ideas. "If you go down on me right now, I'm not going to last long enough to fuck you. And now that you're here...now that this is a thing...I want it all. I need to be buried inside you. Now."

Andi flashed him a wicked grin. Then she spun to face one of the metal shelving units to her right. She put her hands on the shelf at hip height, then bent over, spreading her legs even as she settled into place. "Come and get it, Simon."

He did.

Simon put his hand on the small of her back and pressed until she was at precisely the right angle for him to guide his cock to her saturated pussy. He rubbed the blunt head up and down, coating it in her juices and rekindling some of her arousal. She loved it when they ran their cocks up her slit, nudging her clit.

Today was no exception.

Andi moaned and lowered her head to her forearm, biting it to keep from groaning any louder as he began to prod her still-clenching opening. When he pressed forward, slipping the barest bit inside her, her knees wobbled.

The movement sent him off course. His cock veered from its target and glanced across her ass. They both grew tense. He grabbed his dick and repositioned it, this time notching the tip inside her for only a moment before burying himself a few inches deep.

Usually he was gentle with her. Sweet, and carefree.

Today was something else. Something a little more urgent.

Simon loved that she'd come to him, that she was here in his domain. That he didn't have to hide...well, other than not fucking out in the common area. But the guys would know. Gossip travelled faster in a locker room than in the tiny town he'd grown up in. And he couldn't say he minded.

With that thought in mind, Simon wrapped his hands around Andi's tiny waist. He anchored her while he penetrated farther and farther into her body, until they were fully connected. He stayed like that, buried within her, for a moment to allow them both to adjust to the overwhelming sensations.

He leaned over to kiss her shoulder lightly before planting his feet, standing upright, and getting to work. Simon fucked Andi with long, deep strokes then a few shorter ones that pressed the head of his cock over her G-spot. He watched her ass clench as he hit the right place, thinking of how turned on Reed and Cooper would be if they could see how perfectly she responded to him. Later he'd be sure to tell them all about it and watch what happened when they no doubt went in for some fun of their own.

He began to move faster as he thought of it, of how beautiful Andi would look trapped between them and how incredible she felt as she smothered his cock with her pussy.

She pushed her ass back against him, letting him know she was getting off on his rougher-than-usual treatment. It shouldn't have been a shock to him, given how she liked to fuck Reed and the games they often played, but he hadn't realized that she could bring out a part of him he hadn't ever known existed before.

Simon tried not to growl as he staked a claim on her. One that went deeper than any he'd felt before. He rode her furiously as they both reached for an orgasm that could be snatched away at any moment should someone come knocking or the players finished their meeting earlier than anticipated.

Andi saved him from that terrible fate. She tightened around him, nearly strangling his cock, then came hard. Her channel spasmed and undulated, ensuring that he went over with her. Simon pumped his release deep inside her, making sure to flood her with his seed, hoping that she knew how utterly she possessed him and inspired him to reach new heights both sexually and in his life in general.

He bent over her, wrapping his arms around her as he continued to lunge with deep, hard strokes, until both of them were panting and goose bumps broke out on Andi's arms.

He pulled out, groaning when the cool air of the supply room smacked his dick. Compared to her warmth and the softness of her body, it was a shock. Before she could straighten up, he grabbed a handful of terrycloth from the stack of neatly folded towels and cleaned Andi up, ensuring she wouldn't have any embarrassing accidents on the way out or during the game.

He sure as hell hoped she'd think of him while she was sitting up in the stands between Cooper and Reed.

"That was...amazing." She sighed and laid her head on his shoulder.

"It was."

"But now you have to get back to work." Andi checked her skirt and the rest of her appearance as best she could in the distorted reflection on a glass-fronted cabinet.

"You look incredible," he promised her.

"I look well-fucked." She grinned.

"Isn't that what I said?" He kissed her one last time, at least for now, then put his hand over the lock. He wished they didn't have to go back out to the real world.

"Go ahead." She touched his arm lightly. "In a few hours we'll be home and we can take all night if you want."

He nodded and opened the door. When they were a few feet away, in the middle of the treatment area, Simon took Andi's purse and stealthily transferred her panties from his pocket into it. He leaned down to whisper in her ear, "When you get back to the stands, slip those to Reed. Make sure he shows Cooper, too."

"They'll be hard the entire rest of the night. You know they will." She put her hand over her open mouth. "You're so mean."

"Never. I'll let him and Cooper have you first when we get home." Simon kissed her cheek. "Seems only fair. Now...be careful around breezes."

Andi's cheeks probably would have turned rosy if they weren't already pink from their liaison in the supply cabinet.

"I love you, Andi. You know that, right?" He smiled as he leaned his forehead against hers. Their stolen moments were just about over. He could hear the players breaking up the huddle in the locker room.

She sighed. "Yep. I do. And I love you, too. Now, I should let you get back to work."

As much as he'd like to argue, she had a point.

"Hey, kid. Aren't you going to introduce me to this lovely lady?" A booming voice ricocheted off the cement floors and cinderblock walls of the players' space.

Simon lifted his head. He tried to remember where he was, and figure out who was interrupting his goodbye with Andi. Ah, *that* guy. He was kind of a tool, but too important to give the finger to just to steal a few more seconds with his girl. He gestured to the newcomer. "This is Marty Schone. He's a fancypants lawyer that keeps our guys out of too much trouble when they do something dumb. Marty, meet my girlfriend, Andi."

When Andi didn't respond right away, and neither did Marty, Simon wondered what he was missing. The two of them sized each other up for half a second before Marty cleared his throat and extended his hand. "Uh...nice to meet you."

Andi's face was pale as she reached out and took it in an awkward shake. "Likewise."

Except the way she said it made Simon think it was anything but *nice* for her. What the fuck was going on? He didn't like the panicked look in her eyes or the way she started scoping out the exit, so he stepped in front of her, putting himself between Andi and Marty. "I was about to walk Andi out. I'll see you later, huh?"

Simon slapped Marty's shoulder a little harder than necessary. Then he wrapped his hand around Andi's, which might as well have been a block of ice. Moments before she'd been so very, very warm. He curled his arm around her shoulders and led her toward the exit as quickly as he could without appearing suspicious.

"What the hell was that about? Do I need to kill that guy?" Simon asked in a low, stern tone he didn't even know he was capable of making. He guessed when it came to Andi and keeping her safe, there were instincts that had only been triggered once before in his life. The night she'd been assaulted.

"No. It's nothing." Her wan smile didn't reach her eyes. He'd much preferred the way they'd looked a few minutes ago when she'd barely recovered from her orgasm. "I mean, something, obviously. But we can talk about it later. After you're done working. At home."

"Are you sure?" Simon ignored the shout from his boss, telling him he was needed and his break was over.

Andi nodded. "I'm going to go find Reed, okay? I'm sure he's still in the hallway right over there."

"Text me as soon as you're back together, please." Otherwise he'd never be able to concentrate. The last thing Simon needed was to be distracted and fuck up a key athlete's throwing arm or some shit like that.

Andi leaned in as if she was going to hug him or kiss him goodbye. Instead she lifted her hand in a limp wave before spinning on her heels and darting out the door that led to the main parts of the stadium.

A few moments later his phone buzzed, letting him know she'd reunited with Reed, who would ensure no physical harm came to her. Could he do anything to stop whatever had upset her, though?

Simon turned his attention to his players. His stomach was in knots the rest of the night, despite the fact that they crushed their opponents due to several glorious moves by the player he'd treated with an experimental technique earlier. Even worse, Marty Schone was nowhere to be seen. So Simon had to wait hours to find out what the hell was going on.

If it turned out that Andi had recognized Marty from

Flesh, if the man had anything at all to do with the incident last year, Simon wouldn't be nearly as friendly the next time they bumped into each other.

"Is this a massage or are you trying to beat me up?" the player he was working on post-game joked. "You're supposed to chill out after you get some. Especially from a woman like the one Jerome saw you sneaking out of the supply closet with. Maybe you're not doing it right. I could give you some pointers if you need a bedroom playbook..."

"Fuck you. We're doing it just fine." Simon was afraid that might be the only thing they were doing right in their relationship at the moment. After waiting months for Andi and the guys to come hang out at his work, he suddenly couldn't wait to go home instead.

8

Cooper had been preparing for this moment since Andi had rushed back into the stands at the Sabertooths game and insisted they needed to talk. She'd been so white she had been nearly translucent, and shivering. Only the fact that Reed had escorted her to Simon's domain and back had reassured Cooper that no one had hurt her while she'd been out of his sight.

Except maybe *he* had inflicted damage when he'd claimed her in public that night at Coeur. He couldn't take it back now, and resented the idea that he should have lied about what Andi was to him. It wasn't fair. He'd known people who beat their spouses, cheated on their partners, and yet he had to hide his love for a woman simply because outsiders might not be able to deal with the fact that other guys loved her, too? Bullshit.

Marty stood at the entrance to Cooper's cubicle. Cooper didn't rate an office yet, since he was only an intern. His boss asked, "Could I talk to you for a moment?"

"Sure, what's up?" Maybe it wasn't what he thought.

"I'd rather wait until we have some privacy to discuss it," Marty said. "Step inside my office, please."

Shit. It was *exactly* what he thought.

So Cooper filled his lungs to nearly bursting as he rose from his desk chair, straightening his suit jacket as he did so there wasn't anything Marty could find fault with. Other than his unconventional relationship, that was.

Marty made small talk, asking about Cooper's weekend and dumb stuff like that, until they'd shut themselves into his office. When Cooper mentioned that he'd gone to the Sabertooths game, Marty's eyebrows practically launched themselves onto the roof. "You were there?"

"Yeah. It was a good one. Wish they hadn't left it until the final seconds of the game to secure the win, though." In truth, he'd hardly seen the match-up since he'd spent the entire time trying to convince Andi that she didn't need to hide behind the giant foam finger he'd bought her while picking up their hot dogs and beer.

It had ripped him up to see her that unsure again. Over the past year, she'd really come out of her nerdy bookworm shell and blossomed. He hadn't realized exactly how much until that moment. And he'd do anything to make sure she didn't regress.

"I know, right?" Marty chuckled before jamming his hands in his pockets, crumpling the edges of his suit jacket in the process. "Well, about that...I was there, too. Are you still with that girl, Andi?"

There it was. And he wasn't about to lie.

"Yeah." Cooper nodded. "She's the love of my life."

"I'm sorry, man. I don't know how to tell you this..."

Marty drew a deep breath, then confessed, "Your girlfriend is cheating on you."

"She's not." Cooper shook his head.

"Ah, shit." Marty ran his hand through his hair. "I debated saying anything, but I saw her with another guy at the game. He also called her his girlfriend and it looked like they'd just had one hell of a good time in the medical supply closet under the stadium."

"I know." Cooper left it at that.

Marty sat down hard in his plush leather chair. "What? What do you mean, you know?"

"Simon and I are roommates. We both date Andi." Cooper only then realized how inadequate those words were. They didn't date her. They *loved* her. If they were a traditional couple they'd be engaged or maybe even married by now. Instead they were still...dating. Lame. "So does our other roommate, Reed."

"Wow. That's..." Marty held his hands balled, one near each temple, then expanded them, his fingers mimicking an explosion. "Are you serious?"

"It works for us." He shrugged. "I appreciate you looking out for me, though."

Case closed, right?

Apparently not. Marty suddenly seemed to have a million more questions. They were lawyers. That's sort of how they were programmed to work. Still, Cooper didn't see the merit in it when he'd done nothing wrong and it was his privacy the guy was invading.

Cooper wasn't a damn criminal on cross-examination. He was a guy who had a very complicated, very consensual romantic arrangement with a woman and her other two lovers. So he shut Marty down. "Are you asking as my boss or a random guy I know? If it's the latter, sorry,

I don't kiss and tell. If it's the former, frankly, I'm not sure how my personal life impacts the work I do here."

Marty blinked a few times, as if he hadn't expected Cooper to be so direct.

Tough shit. When it came to protecting Andi and the bond they shared, he would go up against anyone to make sure nothing endangered that.

"Whether or not it's fair, our staff needs to maintain a certain level of decorum. We represent some of the most high-profile people in our community. If it gets out that one of our lawyers—or even some peon intern—has done something immoral or uncouth, it reflects on the firm. It could even look bad for our clients. They won't hesitate to drop us if they sense we're going to draw more attention to whatever legal troubles they're having, which are often damaging enough to their reputations on their own." Marty leaned in. Suddenly, it was easy to see why he had a reputation as a shark in the courtroom. "Look, I'm not telling you what to do, but it would be better for your career if you found yourself another girl. One who is yours and only yours."

"I appreciate your advice." That didn't mean he was going to listen to what Marty said, though. Never. Cooper was *never* giving up on Andi or the rest of their little cohort.

Before he could make that clear, Marty shocked the hell out of Cooper. "Of course, if you'd like to pass her over to me for a bit, let me in on the fun, I could probably think of a way to consider this confidential. Even keep the partners off your back. Maybe write you up some kind of—"

"Did you just suggest that I whore my girlfriend out?" Cooper could feel his knuckles locking into place. He'd never resorted to physical violence before, not even that night in Flesh, when they'd interrupted the heinous assault on Andi.

Today could be a first.

"What's the big deal?" Marty shrugged. "You obviously don't have a problem with her banging other guys. Hell, I'll even let you watch if that's your thing."

"First off, boss or not—fuck you. Second, I don't decide who Andi sleeps with. She does. And no way in a million years would I let you touch her when you want her for all the wrong reasons. She's not a toy." How could he make someone see the difference between what he shared with his roommates—a term that was irking him more and more with its woeful inadequacy—and what Marty was proposing?

Because to him, the two were nothing alike.

Another seed of worry planted itself in his gut. What if there came a day when Andi wanted to bring someone else into their circle? How would he feel about that? What if that person didn't love her like he, Simon, and Reed did?

Did she and the guys assume like he did, that they were complete?

Cooper realized there was a lot they had glossed over, too much they'd been hiding from. Not only public displays, but also within the confines of their own relationship. Technicalities they needed to sort out before someone got hurt.

"Hey, hey. No need to get upset." Marty held his hands up, palms facing Cooper. "I didn't mean any disrespect."

Cooper doubted that, but he was also smart enough to know it'd be bad to punch his boss in his stupid fucking face. He barely made it out of the office before he said something he couldn't take back. Something that would absolutely lead to his termination.

He sat in his cube, fuming but working diligently until it was time to go home.

Then he took the long way, wondering what the hell he was going to say to the people who'd become his family. How the hell were they going to make this right? What would he do if they couldn't?

9

———

When Cooper reached their apartment, he stood in front of the door for a few moments, afraid to go inside. Whatever happened next was going to determine the path of his future. What if it didn't go in the direction he hoped?

He might have hesitated even longer if he hadn't heard a muffled groan.

With a twist of his wrist, he stepped inside and found that it had been a sound of pleasure, not one of pain. Cooper realized then that Andi's molestation had impacted them all, more than they'd admitted to themselves.

He was simultaneously relieved to find his roommates safe and more worried that they might be too tangled up in complications to find their way free. He took off his coat and set his briefcase on the floor near his shoes, which he'd toed off.

Then he stood there, admiring the way Reed and Simon fit with Andi.

Simon was lying on the couch on his back while Andi

straddled him. She rode him while Reed cupped her breasts from behind. He plumped them, pinching her nipples and biting the nape of her neck until she begged him to fuck her, too.

It had only been a week or so since they'd triple-teamed her in the hotel. This was her new favorite way to play. He knew they'd make room for him, too, if he wandered between them. He didn't.

Cooper tensed as Reed did as she asked. Reed retrieved a bottle of lube from the drawer in their coffee table then used it to slick his hard-on. Andi's ass was next. It glistened before Reed smacked it, making Andi moan and Simon curse. She must have squeezed his cock with her pussy as the sharp sting of Reed's palm traveled through her.

It said something that the three of them didn't even notice him ogling them.

He stayed long enough to witness the powerful moment when they connected, as Reed eased himself inside Andi's body, making sure she felt nothing except pleasure. Seeing the three of them joined—making each other feel so damn good it made his own socked toes dig into the hardwood floor—well, he knew he had some tough decisions to make.

How could he give that up? Cut himself out of experiencing it for the rest of his life?

They would be okay without him—look at them...

But could he survive without them?

Cooper balled his hands into fists and marched past the trio, heading toward his room. He couldn't remember the last time he'd spent the night in there, alone. Tonight would be the first in a while.

He needed to think. Needed to get away from the

temptation brought on by the sights and sounds now behind him. Of course, Reed wasn't about to let him escape that easily. Once Cooper had passed the guy, entering his field of vision, he called out, "Aren't you going to come over here for a better look? Maybe give us a hand?"

Cooper had to admit, any other time, he would have.

"Looks like you're doing a pretty good job on your own." He shrugged one shoulder and willed himself not to stare. If he did, he might get sucked into their good time. That would only makes things harder when he came clean about Marty and his job and how he might have to go back in the poly-closet after they'd only just resolved not to sneak around like this was wrong anymore.

Fuck. He wouldn't blame Andi if she kicked him out for backtracking like that.

Cooper ignored Simon and Andi's escalating moans and what it could mean for him if he just gave in to temptation and joined them, like usual. He stomped to his room and slammed the door. It didn't feel like a sanctuary, though. It felt foreign.

Usually him and the rest of the guys shared Andi's personal space. She didn't seem to mind in the least. In fact, she would usually come find one or all of them when she was ready to go to bed for the night. None of them enjoyed sleeping alone anymore.

Cooper crashed into the stiff, perfectly made bed, which was far less comfortable than the crumpled sheets and covers of Andi's. He grabbed an overstuffed pillow, which hadn't yet been properly mashed down by too many people resting on it. With a curse, he drew it over his head and tried to muffle the escalating sounds of rapture drifting in from the living room.

His cock didn't get the message. It got harder and harder the longer he listened to how much fun his roommates were having. It did not approve of hiding in the dark while they were out there, really living.

Shit.

He compromised. Still refusing to get up and head back to Andi, he instead unbuckled his belt and opened his pants before slipping his hand into them. He groaned as his fingers wrapped around his shaft and began to stroke, picturing Andi sandwiched between Simon and Reed, loving every moment.

He knew if he'd given her a chance, went and stood by her side, she would have turned toward him and taken him into her mouth. Cooper could have been getting an incredible blowjob right then instead of jerking himself off in the shadows.

That would only dig him deeper. What would happen when he had to face reality again, outside this little bubble where all that mattered was how much they cared for each other?

Damn it! Cooper's dick chose that moment to deflate. He let go with a snarl and flung his hands out, letting them flop onto the bed. Useless.

It was then that he realized the moans and slapping of flesh on flesh had ceased. At least he wouldn't be tortured by them anymore. He closed his eyes, exhausted. Maybe he could fall asleep and stay unconscious for a while.

Nope.

A light though insistent knock came at his door. "Cooper? What's going on?"

Andi. He wondered how long she'd stand out there before she gave up.

"I'm not going away until you tell me what's wrong." Great, she could read minds, too.

He still couldn't bring himself to answer, to give her permission to come in, only to break her heart.

"Cooper, seriously." Her voice was sterner than before and held a note of fear along with her determination. "Are you okay? Answer me, or I'm coming in to check on you."

"Andi, he's fine. He looked...upset. Not sick or anything like that." Reed this time.

Avoiding them was pointless. It would only delay the inevitable, and freak them out more in the process.

"I'm going to see for myself." Andi opened the door a crack. "Cooper? If you don't want to talk, tell me to go away. I need to know you're all right."

"I'm..." Fine? No, he wasn't. "Not dead."

"Oh, okay." She froze, unsure of whether to back out or keep coming.

"You can come in. All of you." He ditched the pillow and sat up, feeling like he'd aged a hundred years since he'd left that morning.

Andi flew to his side, brushing her fingers through his hair as she crawled onto the bed beside him. "What happened today?"

"Turns out Marty is a scumbag. He's going to turn me in for an ethics violation. I mean, unless you want to fuck him to shut him up. In that case, he'll look the other way."

"I'm going to kick his ass," Reed snarled from the door.

Simon put his hand on Reed's shoulder, keeping him pinned in place. "No, you're not. He's not going to touch Andi. And you're not going to jail over some loser. I think I'll have a few words with Coach, though. Doesn't sound like someone the Sabertooths need representing their organization."

Who knew Simon would be the most levelheaded when the shit really hit the fan? Huh.

"Hang on. You're saying you're going to lose your job if you don't break up with me?" Andi clutched her stomach. "You can't give up on your dreams. You've worked so hard—"

"It doesn't mean anything without you. All of you." Cooper scanned across three very worried faces. "Fuck it. If I have to give up my job, my career, anything and everything for you, I will gladly do it."

"No!" Andi shook her head and plopped from her knees onto her ass a few feet from him. "I won't let you."

"You'd rather cut me loose?" Cooper felt sick himself. "You'll still have these two. I guess that's enough for—"

Reed stopped him cold. "That's not what she meant."

"Of course it's not." Andi put her hand on her hip. "It's just that I don't want to be responsible for stealing something that important from your life."

"Nothing is more important than you. This." Cooper shrugged, his mind instantly made up. It was simple, really. If he couldn't have everything he wanted, he'd have to be happy to keep the things that mattered most. "When I go in tomorrow, I'll talk to the partners and tell them where I stand. If I'm not the kind of person they want in their firm, then fine. I'll move on."

"There has to be some other way to get the experience you need." Simon tapped his chin. "We'll figure something out. Besides, once you pass the bar and open your own practice, it won't matter anymore."

"It might to clients. What Marty said made sense. They might not want my actions tarnishing their already sullied reputations." Cooper had to accept the very real possibility. Weigh out his idealism against practical considerations. "I want to say I don't give a fuck, but...it's a lie. I do. It's pissing me off, because it's so unfair. For a lawyer, that's hard to stomach."

Andi took his hand in hers and snuggled up close to him again. "I'm so sorry. The world sucks sometimes. I can't fix it, but we could try to distract you until you calm down and can think about how to handle this with a clear mind."

"You know, I'm beat from..." Reed gestured with his thumb over his shoulder toward the living room. "I think I'm going to turn in early."

Cooper raised a brow at him. Reed smiled, letting Cooper know he could tell he needed some alone time with Andi.

"I could go again." Simon cracked his knuckles.

"Idiot." Reed snagged Simon by the neck and dragged him toward the door.

Simon's eyes widened. "Ohhhhh. Yeah, sorry. See you in the morning." He waved lamely before shutting the door behind him, leaving Cooper alone with Andi.

"You don't mind? You can call them back if you'd rather..."

"You need me more right now," Andi said softly before kissing his chest over his heart.

Could she feel it racing? Did she know it was cracking open at the thought of losing her, this?

Probably. Because she was careful with him as she pressed his shoulders and guided him back onto the bed, then straddled him so that she could brush her lips over his. She kissed him gently, sweetly, infusing as much care and comfort into her caresses as possible.

He ate it up. His arms went around her, clinging to her as he kissed her back.

Her hands slipped beneath his dress shirt, struggled enough that he rolled her over and shed his clothing as quickly as possible. Then he returned to her without anything between them, nothing keeping them apart or preventing skin-on-skin contact.

He sighed as he settled over her, his cock falling naturally between her legs.

They rubbed against each other, aligning themselves so that all he had to do was clench his ass, shift his hips toward hers, and his cock began to burrow inside her. They both paused, their stares colliding at that first intimate moment where contact became penetration.

He fit himself inside her and reveled in the heat of her body surrounding him, wet and welcoming. There wasn't anything kinky about how they made love. It was simple. Basic. Pure human connection. And he needed it desperately.

Apparently, so did Andi.

She raked her nails down his back, as if terrified he might fly away if she didn't keep hold of him while he slid in and out of her soothing heat. It lasted a long time, their gentle rocking, pressing, and grinding. Eventually, he felt himself spiraling out of control.

As Andi's body clenched around him, trying to keep him buried deep, he unraveled. He began to fuck her harder, until his vision whited out and all he could do was pursue the passion she inspired in him. He brought them together again and again, thinking in passing that the only way they could fit back together was if he left first, retreating some each time.

Maybe the rest of their lives would be like that, too. If he had to say goodbye for a little while, maybe he could find her again later.

Even that tiny reminder of how fragile their relationship could be spurred him on.

Cooper drove himself inside Andi fully, refusing to allow even the possibility that they could be separated. No. He would not give this up for anyone or anything. Not even his career.

With a roar, Cooper leaned in closer and clamped his mouth on Andi's neck.

He sucked and nipped, marking her, wishing that instead of claiming her, he could somehow show her she'd already done the same to him. Irrevocably.

Andi shuddered beneath him, screaming his name over and over as she came. Her orgasm triggered his own and he poured his release deep inside her, flooding her pussy even as he pumped a few final times.

When he came to rest, with their bodies connected as tightly as possible, he stayed that way, refusing to leave her even if he might be crushing her. Selfish, yes. But he couldn't bear to be separated from her. Not tonight. Not ever.

His mind was made up.

Anyone who didn't approve could kiss his ass, and he'd be sure to tell them that in no uncertain terms. Just not tonight.

Tonight, he wasn't budging from this spot.

Andi wrapped her arms around him and sighed. He rolled to his side and flung his thigh over hers, holding her near as he allowed his eyes to drift shut. She cuddled closer than he thought possible, keeping him warm and comfortable.

His decision made, he slept soundly throughout the entire night and woke well rested, ready to face whatever came next.

10

Cooper felt like he had déjà vu.

He sat in his cubicle after classes the following Monday afternoon and waited for the other shoe to drop. He was certain Marty had told the partners about Andi and what he'd witnessed both at Coeur and that night at the Sabertooths game.

When Cooper had arrived, he'd stopped in as usual to let his boss know he was on the clock. The man wouldn't even meet his gaze and had barely responded. Instead of the usual pile of cases he'd hand off for research or whatever else he needed done, he hadn't had a single bit of work to give Cooper.

So there he was, twiddling his thumbs, spinning back and forth in his desk chair, trying not to go absolutely insane as he waited for someone from HR to can him.

It was even worse than he expected. Before too long, one of the partners' personal secretaries came to fetch him, not the woman who'd hired him or even one of her teammates. This went straight to the top level. Shit, he was really about to get his ass handed to him.

He braced himself, certain of how he had to respond.

This job meant a lot to him, but his relationship meant more. After the weekend he'd spent with Andi, Reed, and Simon, he knew for sure that whatever happened here today wasn't going to break them. He refused to let it.

Maybe he'd switch his law focus to unjust terminations or some kind of human rights work. This was discrimination. Complete and utter bullshit. As a fairly average white male, he couldn't say he'd ever felt this sort of helplessness before, because of something that was simply part of who he was. And no one else should have to either.

Cooper had worked himself into a righteous mental frenzy by the time they approached the conference room. Behind the thick tinted glass, the three partners waited for him, wearing super-serious expressions instead of the easy smiles they usually had for him when they passed each other in the halls.

A light pressure on Cooper's elbow caused him to flinch.

"Sorry, trying to help." His escort smiled warmly up at him. "Relax. They're not that scary, I promise."

While he appreciated the reassurance, Cooper had observed the three men at work both in the courtroom and in negotiations outside of it. They were intelligent, direct, cunning, and cutthroat when they needed to be. He'd admired them. And now he was sure he'd disappointed them.

It sucked having his role models turn on him.

He couldn't put off the confrontation any longer when Ford Westbrook—the partner everyone knew was the unofficial head of the firm—lifted his head and met Cooper's stare. He held his hand out over the boardroom table and curled his fingers toward his palm, beckoning Cooper inside.

Mr. Westbrook's assistant opened the door. Cooper wasn't sure if he could find the courage to walk through it. And then he imagined Andi's face when she'd flown back to the stands after her run-in with Marty. Maybe he could make them see that it wasn't right, wasn't fair, for someone to fear the repercussions of loving someone.

These men specialized in justice. That couldn't sit right with them. Could it?

"Good afternoon, Cooper." Mr. Westbrook stood and shook Cooper's hand.

Cooper found it hard to imagine the man would do that to someone he was about to fire, whose dreams he was about to crush. Then again, he was utterly professional and had fulfilled the rights of criminals at times, treating them with respect as he provided the defense they were entitled to under the law.

Hopefully, the partners didn't see him in the same light.

"Thank you, sir. But I'm not sure that it is. Can we skip the formalities and talk frankly about why you've called me here today?" Otherwise, he wasn't sure he could endure the acid churning in his gut long enough to maintain decorum and walk out of their office with his head held high.

"Of course," Mr. Westbrook said as the man beside him smiled.

"He's a lot like you, Ford," Brady Arman, the second partner in the firm, said. Was that a good thing or a jab among friends? Cooper couldn't tell.

Mr. Westbrook held his hand out to shush Mr. Arman,

but never took his focus off Cooper. "Obviously, we heard from Marty about the arrangement you have at home."

Cooper nodded.

"I'd like to hear more about it directly from you. I'm afraid Marty inserted too much color commentary for me to be sure about the accuracy of what I heard." Mr. Westbrook ignored his third partner—Josh King—when he snorted. He disguised the sound, badly, behind a cough.

"I'm in a loving relationship with a woman, who also openly loves my two best friends. We live together and support each other. Everything we do together is utterly consensual." Cooper stuck to the facts. Lawyers, especially ones as good as these three, should appreciate that.

"I see." Mr. Westbrook plopped into his chair then as Mr. King ran his hand through his blond hair and whistled softly. "Would you please take a seat?"

"Wouldn't it be easier for you to simply send me on my way now?" Cooper sighed. "Marty made it clear to me that the firm has a code of ethics that is strictly enforced."

"We do." Mr. Westbrook nodded.

Cooper jammed his hands in his pockets so they wouldn't see the fists they formed. This was it.

"And that's why we'd like you to sit," Mr. Arman interjected calmly. "We'd like to take a statement from you about your exact conversation with Mr. Schone to be used in case we're sued for terminating his employment, which we will be doing as soon as we have the additional evidence we need to support that decision."

"What?" If Cooper didn't sit then he was going to crash onto the floor like a felled redwood tree. He drew out a sleek leather chair and sank into it, his legs turned to mush.

Mr. King grinned. "He's saying that Marty is a dirty, manipulative piece of shit and we know it. Based on what he told us, we're pretty sure he violated your privacy, displayed an egregious lack of discretion, and insulted your life choices. At worst—"

"He tried to blackmail me with his silence if I'd let him have sex with my girlfriend," Cooper interjected.

"And there it is." Mr. Arman nodded, his face grim.

Mr. King cursed under his breath.

Mr. Westbrook, however, showed only a stony mask. The one Cooper knew he kept in place when he needed to do things by the book to ensure victory. Only right now, he wasn't taking aim at Cooper—as Cooper had thought only moments earlier—but instead at Marty.

What the actual fuck?

Cooper gripped the edge of the table, afraid he might crack a molar if he didn't give his energy some physical outlet right then.

"Does that sound familiar, Kari?" Mr. Arman asked their administrative assistant quietly. Only then did Cooper realize the woman was brushing a tear from the corner of her eye.

She nodded. "He told me he'd keep quiet about what we'd done at the company Christmas party if I didn't raise a fuss."

Cooper's eyes narrowed.

Kari picked at her nail polish before looking directly up at him. "This whole time I've been beating myself up. Wondering how I could have made such a poor decision with a guy I'm not even attracted to. But when I heard Marty ratting you out to Mr. Westbrook, what he was trying to do to you, I realized how manipulative he is. He likes to screw with people's heads almost as much as he likes to fuck them...whether they're into it or not."

"I'm so sorry, Kari. We didn't find out about how he'd cornered you until it was too late to have your blood tested for date rape drugs, but I would bet this firm on the fact that he used chemicals to *persuade* you." Mr. King got up and rounded the table to crouch beside Kari. He glanced over at Cooper before biting his lip.

"Say what you want. I don't mind if Cooper knows the truth." Kari put her hand on Mr. King's and squeezed.

"You didn't do anything wrong. With the two drink tickets allotted to each employee, you sure as shit didn't get drunk enough to suddenly decide you had the hots for that slime bucket and jump his bones in the alley. He used guilt and shame to persuade you that you had. That what happened was at least partially your fault. It wasn't. He raped you. He tried to scam Cooper and his partners in the same underhanded way. That isn't acceptable behavior for one of our staff. And we'd like to make it right."

Mr. Westbrook never took his eyes off Cooper. "Did you hear that?"

"Yes, sir." He definitely needed that hold on the table twice as much now. If he had known this before, he might have been tempted to take that swing at Marty he'd so desperately wanted to the other day. Kari's story wasn't so different from Andi's. Son of a bitch!

"Would you be willing to testify about what you've disclosed today on the record, in a court of law, if it comes to that?" Mr. Westbrook asked.

"Of course, sir." Cooper nodded vigorously enough that he rattled his brains a bit.

"You can cut that shit out." Mr. King chuckled. "He's just Ford to those of us who know him best."

"I don't—" Cooper leaned back.

"Maybe not yet," Mr. Arman said. "But we would very much enjoy getting to know you and your significant others better."

"Go ahead, Ford...blow his mind," Mr. King said as he nudged Mr. Westbrook with his elbow.

"Safe to say you've already done that today. All of you." Cooper glanced over at Kari, who had straightened her spine and lifted her chin. He wished he could hug her, but knew she might not appreciate the contact and definitely didn't need it.

"Well, then, what's a little more TMI between colleagues?" Mr. Westbrook said with the first hint of a smile. "Here's the thing, Cooper. We *are* counting on your prudence in this matter now."

"I'm sorry? I don't plan to hide my relationship with Andi from anyone. We are who we are, and we love who we love. If that's not acceptable—if I and the people I love aren't acceptable—to the firm, then I'll resign. I won't be a part of an organization that refuses to accept us." Hadn't they realized that's what he'd been telling them before?

"I heard you the first time." Mr. Westbrook—*Ford*—grinned to soften the retort. "What I meant is that I'd like to share some sensitive information with you, and I hope you'll understand why it's not exactly public knowledge."

"Oh." The muscles in Cooper's back relaxed. "Yes, of course. I've had a crash course in how damaging it can be when the wrong people find out something about you."

"Exactly." Mr. Arman spoke for the rest of his partners when he said, "I hope you don't mind if we tell you that we're actually quite jealous of you."

"What?" Cooper tipped his head.

"You see, the three of us have been looking for someone like your Andi. We just haven't found her yet." Mr. Westbrook shook his head, grim then.

"It hasn't been for lack of trying, though," Mr. King chimed in. He reminded Cooper of Simon with his fast smile and the flash of his eyes that implied they'd made a lot of women's fantasies come true while they'd been on the hunt for their center. The person who'd belong to them forever.

"Wow, seriously?" Cooper released the table, pressing his palms to the polished wood, finally feeling like maybe —*just maybe*—someone might understand him and what he was going through. Not only as a law student, but also as a person in a polyamorous relationship.

Mr. Arman shook his head. "You're not about to ask him if Andi has a sister, are you?"

Westbrook laughed, then shrugged. "Hey, whatever works."

"Anyway, we decided it was best to tell you, because we want you to feel at home here. Absolutely certain that this disaster doesn't reflect badly on you or your work in any way. It's only been a year since you came onboard, but we'd already decided that we'd like you to stay after you pass the bar, if you're interested." Mr. Westbrook folded his hands, reminding Cooper that he was powerful and far more skilled in negotiations than he was.

Honestly, he didn't really care. He'd been working toward this for years. A spot in a prestigious firm? One where his bosses were onboard with how he chose to live his life? How could he say no to that?

"That's...incredible. Thank you for the vote of confidence."

Mr. Arman said, "You earned it, Cooper. Don't for a minute think we'd make you an offer solely because you're like us. Because you understand what we've learned about how enjoyable it can be to share someone. The two things are completely independent. Both are reasons we think you're a hell of a man, though. And it seems like there will be an office opening up here in the very near future, so you should probably gather up your stuff in your cubicle and settle in more permanently when it's free."

"Wow. I...that's..." Cooper blinked a few times, wondering if he was dreaming. "Incredible. Thank you."

"You're welcome. With that said, we'd love to get to know you better outside of work. We're going on a weekend cruise on our yacht in a few weeks. It's Ford's thirtieth birthday bash. You're invited." Mr. King threw it out there like it was no big deal to hang out with three high-powered lawyers on their massive boat. Cooper had drooled over the photos of the vessel in the lobby.

"I would love to. I just need some time to process all this and talk to Andi and the guys about our schedules." Could this seriously be happening? His roommates would be so happy for him. He couldn't wait to share how the day had gone with them.

Hell, they'd been nearly as wrecked as he was when he'd left this morning. Maybe more.

"Please do. Hopefully they'll also be available. We'd love it if you'd bring Andi and your other roommates with you. We would very much like to meet them." Mr. Arman smiled.

"I'll try to keep Ford from pestering them with too many questions about how you found each other and how things work between you, but you know what he's like." Mr. King rolled his eyes.

"Are you kidding? We haven't gotten to share much about this part of our lives. You're not likely to get us to shut up once we start gushing about Andi and how amazing things have been over the past year." Cooper couldn't wait to rave about it.

"Yep. Jealous, kid. With a capital J." Mr. Arman shook his head and stared out at the city.

"She's out there, Brady," said Mr. King softly. "We'll find her."

"We're not getting any younger," he responded.

"No, but we *are* getting richer," Josh laughed. "So at least we'll be able to spoil her when she shows up."

"She's going to be one lucky woman," Kari beamed at her bosses.

Ford sighed, then stepped forward, extending his hand. "Thanks again for helping us get the proof we needed to lock down Marty's exit from the firm and cover our asses. We really are looking forward to getting to know you and your significant others better."

Cooper loved the way that sounded. Not just the networking and hanging out with people he admired part. But the *significant others* part. He'd never said that aloud to anyone, and he couldn't wait to start.

But first, he thought he should go home and make sure Andi, Reed, and Simon understood that this fire had been lit inside him. Now that it had been, it would never go out.

11

———

Andi peeked out the window for the four-thousandth time in the past fifteen minutes. Nope, that car going by wasn't Cooper pulling in their damn driveway either.

She squeaked when Reed laid his hand on her shoulder.

"Sorry, I didn't mean to scare you." He brushed his thumb over the knotted muscles there. "I'm sure he'll be home soon."

"Come on. Sit down," Simon called to her from the couch.

He opened his arms and she flew into them, settling onto his lap. "Sorry, I know you guys are worried, too. I'm sure I'm not helping."

"You know what you told us the other night? In the hotel?" Reed sat next to them and brushed her hair from her face so he could stare into her eyes. "About how you're afraid we're going to break up?"

She nodded, biting her lower lip to keep it from wobbling.

"It's not going to fucking happen," Reed promised.

"That means he has to choose." Andi sagged, settling closer to Simon, who held her tight. "Us or his job. He loves both."

"One more than the other." Simon sounded nearly as stern as Reed. "It's his choice. You have to let him pick, and I'm sure he's not walking away from this."

"He'll hate me—"

"He won't." Reed said it before she'd even finished. "You didn't put him in this position, remember that. The ignorance of others did. No matter what happens today. It's not your fault."

That was harder to believe.

Andi tried. It still tangled her guts up to know that Cooper could be hurting right then—because of her, indirectly or not—and she couldn't stop it. All she could do was wait for him to come home and give him everything she had in her heart and hope it was enough to make up for his loss.

Her foot jiggled on the sofa until Reed covered it with his hand.

They might have gotten into an argument, or ended up with him tying her to the bed to keep from escalating the apprehension he must have also been suffering from, except just then headlights illuminated the window.

"He's here!" Andi would have bolted to her feet if Simon hadn't held her closer.

"Let him come to us," Reed cautioned. "He might need some time."

"Oh." She hated that he was right. The distance between them might already be forming.

When Cooper's key turned in the door and he opened

it quietly as usual, then calmly took off his shoes and set his briefcase beside them on the floor like he always did, Andi felt her entire soul being ripped out of her body. Why wasn't he saying anything? Why wouldn't he look at them?

It was happening. Just like she'd dreamed in her nightmare.

Except then he turned to face them, and when he lifted his head, his gorgeous wide smile was impossible to miss. He was so damn sexy it hurt. Especially right then.

"Everything okay?" Reed asked cautiously, as if the reaction might be that of a man pushed over the edge into madness.

"Yeah. Amazing, actually." Cooper seemed several inches taller than he'd been leaving their house that morning, the weight of their decisions heavy on his shoulders.

"You told them to fuck off and it felt incredible, didn't it?" Simon asked, speculating just as Andi was about the source of Cooper's unexpected joy.

"It did." He nodded. "Even better, they didn't fire me."

"They didn't?" Andi couldn't be contained then. She squirmed free of Simon's grasp and launched herself at Cooper. "Oh, thank God."

He caught her when she snaked her legs around his waist and her arms around his shoulders. His wide hand cupped her ass, keeping her close. "Actually, I think I got a promotion. Or at least a job offer. They said they want me to come on fulltime once I'm done with school and the bar."

"Seriously? That's great," Reed said as he and Simon came to stand beside them.

"Oh yeah. And it turns out the partners at my firm are living the poly life, too." Cooper grinned, loving their shocked reactions. He set Andi carefully on the ground and explained exactly what had happened.

"I *so* want to meet them." Andi smiled at him. "Can we please go sailing with them?"

The rest of the guys nodded or shrugged. Cooper agreed, "Sounds good to me."

"In that case..." Reed met each of their gazes, relief shining from his eyes. "Let's fucking celebrate."

Key word...fucking.

Andi was down for that. After spending the entire day in a ball of coiled nerves, she needed an outlet for all that energy. As one, they headed for her room, the one with the gigantic bed.

When they'd gotten there, Cooper paused, his hands hovering over the buttons of his dress shirt. "I guess I want to say one more thing first, before we erase how we all felt this morning from our memories."

Uh oh. He had his serious face on again.

"What's that?" Andi asked.

"There isn't a way to express how I feel about you. I mean, I love you. Of course I do. But that doesn't seem like enough. If we were in a traditional relationship, I'd have popped the question by now. You know that, right?" He grimaced.

Wow, she'd never really thought of it like that. She imagined how he might propose, and for a moment felt a twinge of sadness that they'd never have that experience to share with their kids or grandkids. Aw, hell, would she even ever have kids?

She was still young enough, involved in pursuing first

her degree and now her career, that she hadn't thought much about it. Maybe she should, before they finished this discussion and while they were still actively planning their future together.

"It's funny you say that." Reed turned to Cooper and put his hand on the other guy's shoulder. "Hang on."

Reed jogged from Andi's room to the one he sometimes used when he needed his own space. She heard him sprinting down the hall and back in a matter of seconds.

"What is he doing?" she asked Simon and Cooper, who looked every bit as baffled as she felt.

They didn't have to wait long to find out. He came back in a rush, holding something.

Reed cracked open a worn leather box. It wasn't something fresh from a jewelry store, new and perfect. It was something older and more...well loved...than that. He sank to the floor on one knee as he held it out toward her.

Cooper and Simon came closer for a better look.

"Well, are you going to kneel, too, or leave me hanging down here?" Reed asked the other guys even as he used his free arm to elbow the back of Simon's knee. "This is what we want, right?"

"Hell yes." Simon dropped to the ground hard enough he'd probably have to treat himself for a sprain later.

Cooper was more graceful, as always. Fluid and somber as he joined the other guys.

Andi covered her mouth with her fingers as her vision wobbled. A sheen of tears distorted their handsome faces for a moment before she blinked them away. After all, she didn't want to miss a moment of what came next.

"I've been meaning to talk to the guys about this for a

while, but I don't need to anymore. I know how we all feel and I'm ready to make it official. I mean, as official as we can. This is my grandmother's engagement ring. I know it's not big or flashy—"

"It's gorgeous." Andi leaned in for a closer look. The darkened gold was delicate, a filigree surrounding a just-right-sized diamond. She'd never given a thought to what a wedding ring might look like on her finger. But the moment she saw the antique nestled in that jewelry box, she knew that if she had her pick of any one in the world, this would be the one she chose.

"It's also yours." He plucked it from the velvet cushion and held it out toward her. "If you want to wear it, I hope you know that it's a gift not only from me, but from all three of us."

Cooper and Simon nodded as Reed spoke.

"Today showed me a lot of things," Reed said. "One of them is that we're already fucked."

"That's the worst proposal I've ever heard." Simon shoved Reed, knocking him into Cooper. "What the hell are you saying?"

Cooper steadied Reed and glared at him, though he gave him a chance to finish his thought.

"We're already madly in love. That means somehow, sometime, we're going to get hurt by loss. But I want to make sure that it's when we're old as shit and dusty rather than anytime soon. And hopefully I'll go first." He looked between Cooper and Simon, then up at Andi. "Will you spend the rest of your life with us?"

"Wait, not so fast." Cooper put his hand on Reed's forearm when he reached for Andi's hand. "I get what he's saying, and in a way he's right, but I also want you to know that until that time comes, I'm going to do everything in my power to make you happy. To keep you safe, body and heart. You don't need to be afraid of that."

She nodded, her chest about to explode with the pressure of the love she felt for each of the men before her.

Then Cooper, Reed, and Andi glanced over at Simon.

"Shit, do I have to say something deep, too?" He shrugged. "All I know is that I want to be with you and what we have works. Also, that I'm horny. Is that a wrap?"

Andi laughed even as Reed glared and Cooper groaned.

That was the thing—she loved each of them and their own style. A little of everything kept things interesting. Right then Simon kept her from getting swept away in the current of overwhelming emotions.

She loved him for that.

"Yes," she told Simon.

"Yes, we're done proposing, or yes, you accept our proposal?" Cooper asked.

Andi figured she'd alleviate any uncertainty. She bent down and took his face between her palms. "Yes, I want to belong to you."

Then she kissed him sweetly until the room began to spin.

Reed cleared his throat. So she repeated the gesture with him. Just before their lips touched, she whispered, "And you."

Their kiss was more urgent. More aggressive. And every bit as delicious.

While they were connected, Reed slipped the ring onto her finger. The unfamiliar pressure of the delicate band felt right. Like it was supposed to be there.

When she tore herself away, Simon was waiting

eagerly. She grinned as she approached him and said, "And of course you, too."

"Yeah, it would be boring if you only had these two to hang out with all the time," he laughed.

She wouldn't go that far, but still...he had a point.

Simon didn't let her kiss him quietly. He scooped her up and turned the exchange into something playful and light even as he carried her to the bed. He tossed her onto the thick comforter and mountain of pillows before turning to the other guys.

"I have an idea," Reed said.

"A dirty idea?" Simon asked. "Because those are my favorite kind."

Cooper chuckled, but he didn't disagree.

"Yeah. I guess." Reed smirked. "I want this to last all night. Make it something we're going to remember."

"Today is already a day I'll never forget." Andi looked up at her guys and smiled shyly before inspecting the ring they'd given her again.

"Right. But we can make it even better," he promised her before drawing Cooper and Simon into a huddle. Andi squirmed as she watched them plot how best to bring her ecstasy like Simon's players strategized a winning play.

Reed slapped Cooper and Simon on the backs before separating them. Whatever clothes they had on between them hit the floor in the next few seconds. Then the only thing Andi could concentrate on was having them closer.

She reached out blindly, wrapping her hand around whoever she found first. Simon. He groaned and arched into her hold, thrusting his cock between her fingers.

Andi wasn't surprised in the least to find him hard now that she felt like they were on solid ground. With her other hand, she fished around until Cooper took her fingers and guided them to his shaft on her opposite side. The guys were kneeling beside her. Which meant Reed...

A moan left her lips as he pressed her legs apart and slid between them.

"We're going to make love to you together, Andi. Each of us fucking you until he's about to come, before giving someone else a turn. We're going to watch you fly apart over and over, but we're not going to let ourselves do the same. Not until you've had as much as you can take. Does that sound like fun?" he asked, knowing damn well it did.

When she found herself incapable of agreeing, he hesitated, his fingers playing with her pussy, spreading her arousal over her flesh until it was slick and ready for him to find his way home again.

"Tell me you want us," Reed insisted.

"So bad. All of you." She nodded, letting her wanton gaze do the begging for her as it scanned down his torso until it landed on his thick cock.

Cooper's cock twitched in her grasp and Simon thrust his hips at her other hand before adding, "And in case he wasn't clear, we want you to come. As often as you can. We want to give you every shred of pleasure we can."

She turned her head to smile at him. "Roger that."

Her joking mood vanished, however, when Reed took advantage of her distraction to set himself at her entrance and begin to advance. He spread her open, making her clutch each of the other guys tighter in response to the pressure and heat he created between them.

Rather than hurt them, her grip seemed to turn them on. Cooper stared at the place where Reed disappeared within her. He swallowed hard as Reed buried himself deeper and deeper. Andi felt full, not only because of Reed.

This was where she belonged. And where she could envision herself for the rest of her life. That confidence and security gave her the freedom to enjoy what they were offering both for that sinful night and for the future.

Andi cried out, "Yes!"

She planted her heels on the mattress and lifted her hips in invitation, helping Reed to work himself inside her completely. When their bodies rested together, he took a moment to kiss her with a hint of teeth. The prickle made her clench around his shaft, causing them both to groan.

Cooper nudged Reed's shoulder. "Don't you dare ditch the plan already. Quit laying there and fuck her."

Simon laughed. "You tell him. I mean, the sooner he pulls out, the sooner I get my chance."

Andi whimpered. Although the guys were committed to holding out, she was going to have no trouble showing them how much they affected her. She caressed Simon and Cooper, her hands sliding along their lengths as Reed began to move.

He fucked her with long, slow strokes at first, clearly trying to extend his initial round. But it didn't take long before he quit torturing them both and began to pump within her, causing her muscles to coil.

"Oh shit," Reed growled. "She's getting close and I want to come with her."

"Get out of there." Simon shoved Reed's shoulder.

Cooper moved away from Andi, taking his cock out of her grip. He grabbed Reed's shoulders and physically levered him aside. The sensation of his cock slipping from her body had her moaning at the loss.

"Don't worry. I'm here," Cooper promised as he took

Reed's place. He fit himself to her and penetrated her in a single fluid stroke, highlighting the differences between the two men. He was graceful where Reed was rough. Thorough and attentive.

Andi felt around beside her, her hand gliding up Reed's thigh.

"You'd better give me a minute." He blew out a ragged breath, so she settled for cupping his balls instead. They were hard and clung tight to his body. She massaged them, waiting until he'd regained his composure.

Cooper, however, was ramping up. He ran his hands over her body from her breasts down her stomach until his thumb toyed with her clit. She rocked on the bed as he stood upright and dragged her to the edge of the bed. He hooked one of her knees over his arm, and motioned for Simon to hold up the other, giving himself room to work on her.

Instead of starting over from the beginning, Andi's body picked up where it had left off with Reed. It wasn't long before she could feel herself on the verge of an orgasm, thanks to Cooper's cock combined with his feathery caresses around her clit.

Simon noticed right away. "She's ready."

"You're going to come on him?" Reed asked her, making Andi moan.

It was the best answer she could muster right then, her entire body focused on the pleasure about to rain over her.

"Let us see," he goaded her, though she didn't need any prodding.

Rapture blossomed from the places where she touched each of them. Andi threw her head back and let go of the doubts and worry she'd tucked away inside of her. Instead she replaced it with bliss.

They loved her.

They always would.

They wanted her to be theirs. Forever.

She came around Cooper hard enough that she forced his cock from within her. And in those moments where she was lost to the world, bucking on the bed between three incredible men, Simon took Cooper's place.

When she blinked them back into focus, she realized Cooper was by her shoulder, stroking her hair and telling her how good she'd felt unraveling around him. So good that he couldn't put his hard-on back in her or he'd risk breaking their pact.

Instead, Simon did it for him.

Andi gasped at the pressure on her still twitching muscles, but Simon only grinned and helped her through it with short jabs of his hips that introduced his dick to her bit by bit. The gradual penetration stoked the dying embers of her lust until it was reborn.

Not only did he take her up again, he brought her over the top before handing her back over to Reed. This time, he feasted on her breasts and he ground into her. Now that they'd warmed her up, it seemed she couldn't stop from falling into orgasm after orgasm.

Andi let her mind wander, lost in sensation, including the weight of their ring on her finger. All she did was feel. And it felt so damn good.

She came again, losing track of which man it was giving her pleasure, because the truth was it came from all of them. She touched whatever bits of them she could reach, loving the feel of them surrounding her.

Andi had no idea how long they made love, but it

seemed like it could have been all night, like Reed had promised. Then, finally, his voice cut through the daze of rapture that had overtaken her. "I can't hold back anymore. One, two strokes, and that's it. I'm going to lose it this time."

"Yes, do that." Andi tried to say more but couldn't. She wanted nothing other than for them to come inside her and to know that they enjoyed what they shared every bit as much as she had, and would for the rest of her life.

This time when Reed fit himself to her, she made sure to keep her eyes open.

She stared up at him as he took what she was offering and poured his release deep inside her. His muscles bulged, his control fled, and he gave her everything he had before making room for Cooper and Simon to do the same.

One by one they surrendered, and she took all they had.

Greedy? Maybe. But she didn't feel guilty about it anymore.

Because they also owned every molecule of her.

When they'd finished and fallen into a pile on the bed, she curled up between them. Under, over, and around them in a tangle of limbs. She stared at the ring on her finger, ran her index finger over it again and again, until she believed it was real. Only then did she murmur, "I always thought about myself as being yours. But now I know, for sure, that you're mine, too."

"Forever," Reed promised.

And she believed him. Andi sighed. "Forever mine—I like the sound of that."

"Me, too." Cooper hugged her tight, settling her back against his chest.

"Me, three." Simon kissed the tip of her nose. "Now someone move the fuck over so I can stretch out. I need my beauty sleep."

Andi fell asleep with a smile on her face, her body sated and her heart overflowing. Just like she knew she would every night from then on.

If you want to find out about Cooper's bosses and check in on how Andi and the guys are doing, be sure to read Fourplay, coming soon!

If you want to be notified when it's released, sign up for Jayne's Naught News at www.jaynerylon.com/newsletter

If you missed out on the first story in this duet, check out 4-Ever Theirs for the story about how Andi hooked up with her three roommates in the first place.

One woman. Three dudes. No regrets.

College was supposed to be Andi Miller's training ground for the real world. Instead, it's her final Saturday night in her college-grade apartment, and she's still sheltered as hell. Why? Because of her three adorable roommates—Reed, Cooper and Simon.

Determined to have one date where the overprotective trio doesn't scare the guy off, Andi sneaks out for the night. And almost lives to regret it.

When Reed, Cooper and Simon rescue Andi from a bad situation in the basement of a sex club, they decide it's time for the kid gloves to come off. Since their early college days, they've been not-so-secretly fighting amongst themselves to spark her next smile, her next laugh.

They've already done a lot of surviving together, and

now it's time to thrive. At the risk of ruining a beautiful friendship, the men set out to turn their hands-off live-in arrangement into a weeklong learning experience where they become Andi's sex education teachers.

Except none of them realize their new found intimacy will make it impossible to say goodbye on graduation day.

An Excerpt From 4-Ever Theirs:

"Stop. Stop. I'm going to pee my pants." Andi Miller gasped between bouts of hysterical laughter. She swiped tears from her cheeks as her three obnoxiously adorable roommates demonstrated their best attempts at twerking from various places around their kitchen.

Sadly, Simon could definitely shake his ass better than she could. He put on quite a show from his perch atop their rickety table, threatening to turn it into kindling with sharp swings of his hips. The guy could easily have paid his portion of the rent and then some if he'd gotten a job as a go-go dancer.

"We're only trying to help." Cooper punched Simon in the leg then grappled him to the floor. If she didn't act fast, this could deteriorate into another of their infamous wrestling matches. The last one of those had resulted in the annihilation of a beanbag chair. She was still discovering tiny foam beads scattered throughout their apartment months later.

"I mean, it's not like you've come out of your room long enough to pick up any of our moves in the past four years, with all that studying you insisted on doing. You don't want to get embarrassed on the floor tonight, do you?" Reed asked as he simulated humping a cabinet.

Well, that wouldn't be a problem, seeing as she hadn't quite told them the truth about her destination for the evening. Dance club, hook-up spot—same difference, right?

Their over-protectiveness made her white lie necessary.

Besides, she owed them the same courtesy they showed her when it came to keeping their sex lives separate from their home lives.

The guys never brought women to the apartment. Or at least they hadn't in ages. Not since early in the first semester of their freshman year when one of their one-night stands—to this day, they wouldn't tell her which of them had slept with the poor girl—had tried to make herself some morning-after breakfast and ended up with a black eye courtesy of Andi's fist.

Hey, how was she supposed to have known it wasn't an intruder out there whipping up a frittata before absconding into the night with their meager college-grade possessions? Milk crate furniture might be hot on the black market for all Andi knew. If some of the oomph propelling her swing had actually been fueled by jealousy instead of fear, she'd hidden that pathetic fact as best she could from both herself and her roommates.

Ruining their friendships wasn't on her agenda. She wasn't the sort of girl who knew how to screw around then act like sex had been no big deal. Though she had chemistry with each of her roommates, how awkward would it have been to have followed through on it and slept with one of them?

Takeout and movie nights with the others would never have been the same.

Andi admitted it. She was sheltered as fuck. Though her vocabulary had gotten a hell of a lot more colorful as a result of her co-habbing with this trio of idiots for the past four years, she hadn't done a lot of exploring relationship-wise. After all, she spent most of her free time with Cooper, Reed and Simon. Who would approach her with those three hovering over her, snarling and baring their teeth at any guy who got too close?

God, she was going to miss them.

The thought of giving up their second-to-last Saturday night together had her rethinking her plans. Except this might be her last chance to eliminate her regrets about not having a single fling during her college experience. It would help round out her academic studies and the rewarding social experiment living with three dudes had turned out to be.

This was supposed to be her training ground for the real world.

Now that she'd accomplished the majority of her goals —by graduating at the top of her class and scoring a prime position in her field—maybe she could make some time to fill the emptiness growing inside her as she accepted that she'd be forging out on her own soon. The lack of a relationship hadn't bothered her so much when she'd had school and her roommates' friendship to occupy her.

All of that was changing.

So was she.

Andi wanted to be ready for what came next.

"Was it that good for you?" Simon flashed a wicked smile as he teased her.

"Huh?" She snapped herself out of her daze.

"Our dancing."

"Oh, yeah. Definitely. It was so hot I need to go take a shower." She rolled her eyes and giggled some more as she abandoned the kitchen for their shared bathroom. If she was sweating a little, it was surely from nerves over what she was about to do, not because they'd affected her.

Sure.

She scrubbed herself then spent a while drying and curling her hair before applying what dashes of makeup she owned—a bit of mascara and some nude lip gloss. The whole time, she kept wondering what tonight might be like if she could spend it with someone she knew and trusted instead of gambling on a blind date set up by her well-meaning chemistry lab partner.

Andi bit her lip then harrumphed and fixed the damage, at least mentally reminding herself not to rub her eyes before she could wreck them too. She sighed then rested her forehead on the door, praying for some direction. Was she making a mistake? Or would it be an even bigger one to pursue the foolish ideas tempting her to feel out her roommates about her proposition?

Before she could make up her mind, a rap on the door rattled her brains.

"Ouch. Fuck." She stumbled back.

"Yo, Andi. Quit hogging. I drank three beers with dinner, and I gotta piss," Reed groaned. "I forgot what it's like to wait on someone trying to be girly."

Aaaaaaaaand… That sealed the deal.

They were too much like brothers to ever see her as a woman. Which was exactly how she'd wanted things while they lived together. She grinned as she opened the door. Reed squashed past her in the doorway, wedging them together when he froze. "Damn.

Uh, you look…great."

"The magic of wearing something other than sweats and one of your roommates' old shirts sans a bra." She shrugged.

"I kind of prefer the no-bra part." Simon waggled his brows from where he scarfed another helping of now-cold pizza for second dinner.

When she turned to him with a smile, he paused mid-bite.

"What?" Andi finger-combed her hair as she stepped from the bathroom so Reed could relieve himself in peace. Not that the guys didn't invade her privacy often when she was in the shower, or vice versa. The trials of a single bathroom for four people had absolutely played a part in her collegiate years.

"I told you," Reed shouted through the door.

"They're right. You're hot." Cooper took her hand and spun her around. "I'm not sure we should let you go out like this, young lady."

"Whatever, Dad." She chuckled until he finished twirling her, though it hadn't entirely been a joke. With her parents both gone, these guys had stepped up and filled a huge, painful void as best they could. They were, and always would be, her family.

In the heels Andi had borrowed, she was closer to Cooper's height. Meeting his warm stare, she caught the spark of something serious there.

Could he actually be attracted to her?

She knew each of them appealed to her in various ways—Cooper's gentlemanliness and tact, Simon's playfulness and daring, Reed's sense of responsibility and control.

As if a sliver of possibility was the only prompt her subconscious required, she blurted the thoughts that had been haunting her for the past hour. Okay, longer than that. At least since she'd agreed to this outing. Probably since the day she co-signed their lease.

"Maybe you guys should come out too?" She prided herself on the fact that she only stammered a little when she said, "Or I could stay home and we could have a private party instead."

Simon blinked at her, the pizza still lodged half-inside his mouth.

Cooper's fingers tightened around hers. His other hand landed at her waist to steady her. But he didn't say anything.

The door opening behind her broke the moment, forcing them apart.

Reed emerged as the toilet finished flushing in the background. It was as if her silly dreams circled the bowl then vanished down their clanky pipes when he grimaced. "What's that? Don't back out now. You've been looking forward to tonight all week. It's about time you cut loose. On your own. You've earned this."

"Oh. Okay." If they noticed the tremble in her faux smile, they didn't call her on it.

Andi decided to quit fucking around. Playing a game where she didn't know the rules was a sure way to lose. Reed was right. She had to learn to stand on her own, without leaning on them. Because in a matter of days, they wouldn't be part of her everyday existence anymore.

Graduation was a week away.

Her new life, the one where she'd be a lab tech in a prestigious pharmaceutical research firm—one that didn't include her roommates—was calling.

"Go ahead. Have fun," Simon said around a mouthful of pepperoni. "Besides, we've already—"

Cooper cleared his throat, but it was too late. She realized they must have dates. Of course they did.

"Hey, you'll be fine," he promised. He looked away before adding, "You don't need us."

Andi swallowed around the lump in her throat. She took a step forward and then another before grabbing her wristlet and keys out of the bowl at the end of the countertop.

If she was going to do this, she couldn't linger. Otherwise, she'd never convince herself to leave.

"Be safe!" Reed shouted as she closed the door softly behind her, determined not to let the stinging of her eyes turn into real tears and screw up her mascara.

To keep reading **4-Ever Theirs, click here.**

If you liked reading about this steamy non-traditional relationship, you should check out Nice & Naughty, another of Jayne's menage stories.

Can one man satisfy Alexa's appetites? Or will it take two?

After a disastrous lesson in heartache, Alexa Jones confines her adrenaline rushes to intense boardroom negotiations. Her legendary control cracks and she indulges in a high-octane encounter on the hood of her sports car. She never planned to see the enticing stranger again. When she finds herself across the boardroom table from him, there's suddenly more at stake than just her career.

Justin Winston got more than he bargained for on his summer drive, but he should have known nothing is ever that easy. He's met the woman of his dreams yet he doesn't know who she is. Luckily, he can always count on his practical brother for the things that matter, and this time is no exception. But, when a web of corporate espionage entangles them all, it's clear Justin isn't the only one who's fallen for their mysterious siren.

In Justin and Jason, Alexa finds something as unique and rare as the patent they will risk their lives to secure. The freedom to explore—and satisfy—the full range of her desires. From naughty to nice. Can Alexa accept the love of two men?

Warning: This story contains light bondage, anal play and smoking hot brothers for double the fun and double the trouble.

An Excerpt From Nice & Naughty:

"She's beautiful," he murmured reverently.

The car. He's talking about your car. She tried to convince herself, but the rationalization rang false. While he admired the convertible, something more arced between them. Attempting to shake off the unusual reaction inflaming her senses by focusing on her vehicle, Alexa stepped a little closer.

"I've done a lot of work on it."

"Can I touch her?" His implicit understanding of her dislike for people handling her vehicle made her confident he would treat it with the respect it deserved.

"Sure, go ahead." Plus, she got to watch the way his broad finger stroked the defined contour in the flawlessly waxed side panel, which inflamed her senses nearly as much as if he'd placed the caress on her skin instead.

Before she could stop to analyze what her subconscious offered, she asked, "Would you like to take a look under the hood?"

"Hell, yeah."

She had to laugh at the look on his face. "You look like a kid on Christmas."

"It's not every day I come across an opportunity like

this." The dark undercurrent of the statement and his piercing green stare made it clear he referred to more than a fancy sports car.

Oh God. He feels it, too.

Alexa should have been freaked out. Alone with a stranger, on a deserted stretch of highway, in the mountains far from the city, sounded like an unwise situation to put herself in. She should be nervous but a remarkable calm surrounded her instead. In fact, she just now realized she'd stopped on the side of the road without a second thought to safety. Today, she threw caution to the wind. The chemical reaction between them affected her like a drug.

As though he sensed her train of thought, the man backed away a few steps, displaying his non-threatening intent. He left the path clear for her to get in her car and drive away but her instincts shouted that she could trust him. She wanted to explore this attraction just a little bit further.

She leaned over the door and rested her fingertips on the hood release. The man's gaze tracked her movement yet he didn't encroach on her space. For a moment, the only sounds breaking the silence were the babble of the stream below, the gentle rustle of leaves from the tree branches overhead and a soft birdsong.

The air between them crackled with tension.

Then, the metallic click of the hood's latching mechanism disengaging relayed her decision to stay. A broad smile spread across his face, raising faint dimples that heightened his attractiveness. Alexa inclined her head in a "come here" gesture as she circled around to the front of the car.

He ambled to her side with a steady gait that made her

cognizant of his confidence she wouldn't run. Reaching for the edge of the hood simultaneously, their hands met. Sparks shot up her spine and she jerked. His arm wrapped around her waist in a protective hold. The solid strength kept her from losing her physical footing, but not her emotional balance. This close she could smell the unique combination of his leather gear and subtle, earthy cologne.

"Easy." His hand smoothed down her side and across the top of her ass as he went back to lifting the hood. The blatant touch imbued her with respect for his natural ability to handle a woman. However, she retained enough rationality to admire the gleaming chrome of the engine that she cleaned with painstaking diligence each weekend she could manage the time. Together they leaned forward, caught by the lure of a ridiculously overpowered motor.

"This is an aftermarket addition. Did you do this yourself?" His raised eyebrow conveyed his surprise.

"Yeah."

"I'm impressed. Are you a mechanic?"

"Nope, this is just a hobby." She smirked.

"Some hobby. I *am* a mechanic. This is a damn fine job."

Alexa basked in his appreciation for details. None of her friends understood her devotion to this machine. They couldn't comprehend why she spent the majority of her precious free time refining each tiny part until it was flawless. This man obviously did.

He ran his hand along the connections, searching with deft flicks of his fingertips for imperfections where none existed. His satisfied nod had her beaming.

"Jesus, woman. If someone told me I'd have the chance to play with a car like this today, I'd have said that nothing could distract me. But the way you're looking at me..."

His voice trailed off as she reached up to do a little exploring of her own. Her hand moved on autopilot, following her desire, cupping the side of his stubbled face.

Is this guy for real?

The wet heat of his lips on her palm rasped against her nerves, stronger than any dream. She whimpered as he turned his head to lick the center of her palm before catching the sensitive skin between her thumb and index finger in his teeth in a gentle nip. The move set her ablaze, destroying common sense.

"Kiss me," she demanded.

He didn't need to be told twice. With a low groan, he closed the narrow gap between them, sealing his mouth over hers. He dropped the hood in place and put his hand to better use, wrapping it around her hip, yanking her tight against the hard plane of his chest. His height made Alexa strain on tiptoes to return his kiss. Eager to help, he tucked his other hand around her thigh, just beneath the curve of her ass, and hoisted her up higher on his body.

They fit perfectly together.

Her hands tangled in his hair, loving the way the silky strands teased the sensitive crevices between her fingers. She kneaded his scalp, urging him to take her mouth deeper. His head angled over hers, intensifying the kiss as his tongue lashed playfully against the seam of her lips. She drew it inside her mouth and sucked. He tasted like peppermint.

She moaned with regret when he pulled away.

"I'm going to set you on the hood." He rumbled in her ear in between nibbles of her neck.

"No! Wait."

Though he looked disappointed, he stopped without hesitation.

The heat suffusing her face highlighted her discomfort with being so brazen. "I... I don't want to scratch the paint. Take my shorts off first."

Strained laughter burst from his chest. It transformed his features from rugged to unbearably handsome.

"Honey, you're my every fantasy."

To keep reading **Nice & Naughty, click here.**

NAUGHTY NEWS

Want to win cool stuff? Get sneak peeks of upcoming books? How about being the first to know what's in the pipeline or where Jayne will be making appearances near you? If any of that stuff sounds good then sign up for Jayne's newsletter, the Naughty News. She never shares you information, pinky swear!

www.jaynerylon.com/newsletter

WHAT WAS YOUR FAVORITE PART?

Did you enjoy this book? If so, please leave a review and tell your friends about it. Word of mouth and online reviews are immensely helpful and greatly appreciated.

JAYNE'S SHOP

Check out Jayne's online shop for autographed print books, direct download ebooks, reading-themed apparel up to size 5XL, mugs, tote bags, notebooks, Mr. Rylon's wood (you'll have to see it for yourself!) and more.
www.jaynerylon.com/shop

LISTEN UP!

The majority of Jayne's books are also available in audio format on Audible, Amazon and iTunes.

GET IN TOUCH

Jayne Loves To Hear From Readers

www.jaynerylon.com

contact@jaynerylon.com

Hammer it Home

HOT RODS

Powertools Spin Off. Keep up with the Crew plus...

Seven Guys & One Girl. Enough Said?

King Cobra

Mustang Sally

Super Nova

Rebel on the Run

Swinger Style

Barracuda's Heart

Touch of Amber

Long Time Coming

STANDALONE

Menage

4-Ever Theirs

Nice & Naughty

Contemporary

Where There's Smoke

Report For Booty

COMPASS BROTHERS

Modern Western Family Drama Plus Lots Of Steamy Sex

Northern Exposure

Southern Comfort

Eastern Ambitions

Western Ties

COMPASS GIRLS

Daughters Of The Compass Brothers Drive Their Dads Crazy And Fall In Love

Winter's Thaw

Hope Springs

Summer Fling

Falling Softly

PLAY DOCTOR

Naughty Sexual Psychology Experiments Anyone?

Dream Machine

Healing Touch

RED LIGHT

A Hooker Who Loves Her Job

Complete Red Light Series Boxset

FREE - Through My Window - FREE

Star

Can't Buy Love

Free For All

PICK YOUR PLEASURES

Choose Your Own Adventure Romances!

Pick Your Pleasure

Pick Your Pleasure 2

RACING FOR LOVE

MMF Menages With Race-Car Driver Heroes

Complete Series Boxset

Driven

Shifting Gears

PARANORMALS

Vampires, Witches, And A Man Trapped In A Painting

Paranormal Double Pack Boxset

Picture Perfect

Reborn